W9-DDE-186

Patti Mepham

True to You

WHITMAN BOOKS
FOR GIRLS

"Minnow" Vail

The Charmed Circle

Practically Twins

Then Came November

True To You

That Certain Girl

True to You

By Viola Rowe

cover and decorations by

Celeste Spransy

A WHITMAN BOOK
Western Publishing Company, Inc., Racine, Wisconsin

Produced in the U.S.A.

Library of Congress Catalog Card Number: 64-14754

Contents

1

The Bottom Drops Out

Naturally, the very first thing a girl wanted to do on arriving home from a summer vacation was to telephone her best friend. There was so much to tell, and things to show.

Sally Sorenson wanted to give Sue Fowler the gift she'd brought her from Chinatown in San Francisco. And she wanted to show her the sweater outfit she'd bought for herself while visiting her cousin in Denver. Orange and white it was—their school colors. And Sally wanted to tell Sue about the cute boy who lived next door to her married sister in Portland, Oregon, who had said he would write to her if she wrote to him. And she wanted to tell Sue about swimming in the Pacific Ocean. And about riding in a sight-seeing bus in Hollywood. And so many other things that she felt as if she'd burst if she couldn't get them said soon.

It had been too late when they arrived back in the midwestern town of Linden the night before. And this morning she had slept late. A whole month of vacationing could be tiring, Sally decided as she washed her face and then splashed it with cold water to get the sleep out of her eyes.

Still in her pajamas, she went to the upstairs extension phone in the old-fashioned alcove at the top of the stairs and prepared to be comfortable, propping colorful cushions behind her back as she sprawled on the window seat, taking care that her bare feet extended beyond the chintz upholstery because her mother was fussy about such things as bare feet on clean cushions and pillows.

Lifting the receiver, she was about to dial the number which was still familiar even though she had been away a whole month, when she became aware that their line was already in use. Two men were talking—her father and Mr. Stanton, who had served on the school board with him for several years.

Her father was saying into the downstairs telephone, "I suppose a lot of people in town were upset about it."

Mr. Stanton answered, "Yes, but there just wasn't any other solution to the problem, George. Redistricting was the only answer—"

Sally replaced the receiver and went down the hall to the bathroom to brush her teeth. She had never understood what it was about school affairs that her father and Mr. Stanton found so interesting. Thinking of school, she was not sorry that it was almost time to go back, though of course this was not a thing to be admitted to just anybody. But being a high school sophomore was bound to be even more exciting than being a freshman. This year she would probably be asked to more boy-girl parties. She and Sue might even double-date. That would be fun. Sue was always popping over with ideas, and she made little jokes all the time. Not for the first time, Sally thought how lucky she was to have a best friend like Sue Fowler. And they had been best friends from their kindergarten days—or ever since they were old enough to go back and forth from her house to Sue's, about two and a half blocks away.

To give her father plenty of time to finish his call, Sally eyed herself critically in the bathroom mirror. Her brown hair was too long and needed shampooing. But she liked what all the exposure to sun and wind had done to her. Especially the way it had added interesting streaks to her hair, and made her eyes appear a deeper blue. She considered suggesting that her parents buy a sun lamp so she could keep her tan all winter. With a shrug, she decided that her father was sure to say they couldn't afford nonessentials after their long vacation, even though part of the vacation had been a business trip for him.

She hoped she hadn't gained any weight from all the good meals they'd had everywhere, and decided she probably hadn't, for her clothes weren't snug anywhere. Her cousin Evelyn, in Denver, had said she looked just right in a bathing suit, not too short, not too tall, not fat, but not skinny either. She felt pleased all over again, remembering.

Once more she went to the telephone, and this time another man was speaking to her father. It was someone from his office, asking about the business convention he'd attended in California.

She was hungry, she realized. But if she went downstairs her mother would ask, "Why aren't you dressed,

Sally?" Her mother had definite ideas about some things, and being properly dressed for meals was one of those things. She wondered if she could get away with it if she answered, "I thought we were still on vacation."

While she was wondering, her young sister Lucia came bounding up the stairs. Lucia, who was nine, liked to wear jodhpurs instead of blue jeans, and she loved to pretend that her bicycle was a horse. She was always having "adventures" while riding "Horace," her imaginary horse. Her face was round, like Sally's, and her cheeks were pink with excitement, and she wore her hair in long pigtails. Only on special occasions was she willing to have her pigtails tied with ribbons.

Lucia's greeting was high-pitched with excitement. "Sally, guess what!"

"Okay, what?" Sally asked amiably, sinking back on the cushions of the window seat.

"Have you looked out the window?" Lucia asked breathlessly.

Sally looked, a casual glance. "The sky hasn't fallen. The bottom hasn't dropped out of the world."

Lucia ignored the teasing.

"The carriage-house people have finally moved in!"

she announced triumphantly.

Sally sat upright. What Lucia liked to refer to as "the carriage house" was actually a remodeled old barn behind the house two doors away. Once there had been stalls for horses in that barn, and a place for a carriage—just as there had been in the barn behind her own house, long since converted into a two-car garage plus some storage space. Lucia liked to call their garage "the stable." Her reason for calling the other "the carriage house" was that it was larger, with several rooms upstairs.

Before they left on vacation Sally had learned that a family with three children would be moving into the house two doors away that was so much like their own in outward appearance.

"Have you seen them?" she asked eagerly.

"The new people," Lucia informed her, "have a daughter, a girl, about your age."

Sally laughed. "Daughters are usually girls, Lu. Or didn't you know?"

"And two boys. About my age."

"Good deal! A couple of extra kids for you to play with."

It shouldn't matter too much to Lu whether the new kids were boys or girls, Sally decided; and as for the new girl, it might be convenient sometimes to have an extra girl around. But of course no girl could take Sue Fowler's place.

"Maybe we can see them from my room," Lucia said.

They went to her bedroom at the rear of the house. Here Lucia's love of horses was very evident: There were pictures and drawings, and a Mexican straw horse wearing a gaily patterned wool blanket under his saddle, and figurines in assorted shapes and sizes. Prominently displayed was a photograph of a girl with hair in pigtails, astride a black horse with a splash of white on his nose and legs. The girl in the picture was Linda, their married sister. She had not been much older than Lucia when the picture was taken, and Lucia clung to the hope that one day she, too, would ride her own horse.

For the moment Lucia had forgotten horses. She leaned close to the window screen, looking beyond the adjoining lawn toward the "carriage house."

Sally looked, too. "There's nothing to see." Just a little of the rear of the house and most of the remodeled barn.

"Mrs. Gruenwald says lots of mysterious things were moved into the barn. Nights. Before the movers had even brought the furniture."

Sally's laugh was skeptical. "Mrs. Gruenwald's imagination is as active as yours sometimes." Their next-door neighbor was a widow with no children. She probably didn't have enough to do to keep herself busy, Sally surmised.

Lucia protested indignantly. "It's not imagination. She saw it. With her own eyes."

"I don't doubt she saw things being moved into the carriage house, Lu. But she just imagined that they were mysterious."

"The men came in the dark. And they didn't turn on any lights," Lucia persisted. "And there were so many boxes—"

Sally was becoming impatient with her young sister. "When people move, they put things in boxes. What's mysterious about boxes?"

"Well, they carried them so carefully, Mrs. Gruenwald said. As if they might explode or something. And one man kept watch—"

At that Sally burst into laughter.

"Lu, you're a lulu!" She headed for the telephone again, making a mental note of one more thing to tell Sue: The new neighbors had a teen-age daughter.

The line was free. She dialed the number eagerly.

A familiar voice answered, a pleasantly deep voice that set her heart to beating crazily and threatened to shut off her breathing entirely.

She managed to gasp, "Oh– Hi, Whit. This is Sally."

Ever since her first year in junior high she had been affected this way by Sue's older brother. With most people she managed to converse with reasonable ease. With Whitson Fowler, the one boy in the world she really would like to impress, she stammered and stuttered while every worthwhile word escaped her.

He asked, "How was the vacation?"

"Just great," she answered, and then could think of nothing to back it up.

"Sue's not home."

"Oh," Sally wailed, "she isn't?"

Whit laughed. "Boy, I wish someone was that anxious to see me!"

She could picture him, leaning nonchalantly against the wall in the Fowler hallway, his well-shaped head cocked a little to one side as he laughed, displaying firm white teeth. What would he say if he knew how often she'd thought of him while she was away– or how often she thought of him always? She felt her cheeks warm with embarrassment at the thought of what he might say, if he knew.

But he couldn't know, thank goodness!

Instead, he was saying something about "that slick new chick on your street."

"You've met her?" Sally asked, not at all sure she liked the thought that Whit was already acquainted with her neighbor.

"Not formally," Whitson said, and he laughed again.

She started to say, "Ask Sue to call me—" when he said, "I'll send Sue over pronto when she gets back."

She managed a flurried, "Thanks," quickly adding, "Good-bye."

She hurried to dress, wishing unhappily that she could start the telephone conversation all over. But she probably would do no better, she decided, even though she surely could do no worse!

When she was dressed, wearing blue cotton bermudas and a white blouse, a combination that accented her tan and the blue of her eyes, she went dashing down the stairs, acutely aware of wanting breakfast, lots of breakfast.

She called out, "Morning, Daddy," at the door of the den. Perhaps because of having been away, she was aware of the mellowed look of the room. The leather chairs, the draperies at the long narrow windows, the raisin-brown carpet, even the books on the shelves, all had a pleasantly used look.

Her father looked up from the papers before him on the old knee-hole desk to smile and say, "Good morning, Sally. I don't have to ask if you slept well."

She was halfway down the hall when he called, "Whoa, Sally! I don't suppose you've heard the news?"

"What news?" If it was about that new girl, the one Whit seemed to think was "slick," she didn't want to hear it.

"About the school redistricting that was decided on just after we left."

She wanted her breakfast. She wasn't interested in school news at the moment.

"It means," her father said, "you will be going to the new high school."

All at once she became motionless as a block of marble. Her breath seemed to stop with shock. She forgot about being hungry. Food was utterly unimportant at the moment. She could not believe what her ears had reported.

Her father repeated his words. "You will be going to the new high school. To Hadley West."

Hadley West, the new school that had been built

to accommodate the overflow of students from the subdivisions springing up everywhere, was only a few blocks from where Sally lived. Much closer than the old school. But she hadn't expected to go to the new school. Hadley East, as the old school was now to be called, was her school. It was the school her sister Linda had attended. It was the school she had attended during her freshman year. It was the school she'd expected to graduate from. It was *her* school—the school she loved, though she hadn't thought of it quite that way before. Even though this new school, just barely finished, was so close to home, and was more modern and better equipped—or so they told her, for she had paid it little attention—even if all the good things said about it were true, it just wasn't her school.

Obviously she couldn't go to the new school. She managed to step into the den to make this clear.

"But, Daddy, that just isn't *my* school. I can't go there." She remembered. "I even bought a new sweater set—orange and white—our school colors."

His smile was rueful. People said she looked like him. She liked the way he looked, so she didn't mind resembling him. She didn't even mind that he could be strict at times, because he was often quite understanding.

"I'm afraid we have no choice," he said now. "When the dividing lines were first drawn, they somehow miscalculated the number of children who would be enrolling from certain areas. So they had to be redrawn."

"But—but, Daddy, you can do something about letting me stay where I want to be. You used to be on the school board!"

His answer was firm. "That doesn't give us special privileges, Sally."

She stood there silently for a long while, trying to accept the inevitable with good grace. She could never be loyal to the new school, of course. Her loyalty would always be with the old. But if there was no alternative, then there was no alternative.

With a sigh that had to be hauled up all the way from her gaudily striped play shoes, she said, "Well, at least I'll have Sue there with me."

At that her father rose from behind his desk near the window and came to her side to put his arm about her shoulders.

"I guess I didn't make myself clear, Sally. Sue is on the other side of the boundary line."

That meant Sue would still go to the dear old familiar school!

What she'd said to Lucia earlier just wasn't true.

"The bottom hasn't dropped out of the world," she had told Lucia, jokingly.

But it had. Now she knew. It actually had.

2

Mistaken Identity

Waiting for Sue, waiting to share with her best friend the black misery of her heart, Sally poked restlessly about the kitchen. Her father was still in the den. Lucia had wandered off somewhere. Her mother had gone to the supermarket to buy food to restock the cupboards and refrigerator.

They had brought fresh fruit home with them the night before. Sally was sure she had lost her appetite, but she halved a cantaloupe, and after eating one half, she ate the other. There were a half-dozen or so cookies in the cooky jar, and she ate those. She ate a peach. Then she ate a plum. Then she ate two apricots. Nothing tasted right. How could anything taste right when the bottom had fallen out of her world?

The big kitchen had an old-fashioned air, despite the shining electric range and refrigerator and freezer. All the woodwork was dark, including the glass-paned cupboards, and this made the frilly crispness of the curtains appear even whiter. Until today Sally had thought it a cheerful, as well as a comfortable room. Today it seemed unbelievably dreary as she waited impatiently for Sue.

Hearing the high sound of girls' voices, she dropped an apricot pit into the garbage disposal and hurried out the back door.

It was a still day, with powder-puff clouds dotting a clear blue sky. Sally was scarcely aware of the heat of the August sun against her face as she cut across the back lawn. The Sorenson house was on a corner lot. The voices she'd heard came from the public sidewalk that ran alongside their garage.

Her footsteps slowed as she realized that it was not Sue talking to Lucia, but a stranger. Lucia had propped her bicycle on its metal stand while she and the stranger talked earnestly.

Sally wished she had not come out. This stranger was undoubtedly their new neighbor, the girl Sue's brother had said was slick. Sally eyed her critically and tried to tell herself this girl really wasn't very slick. She was wearing faded blue jeans and a checkered cotton shirt and barefoot sandals. Her black hair was straight and cut close to her head. Yet even with short hair, and wearing jeans, she did not have a boyish look. Though she was not really pretty, there was something about the girl, Sally admitted, thinking of Whit. It was something about the way she held her head, and the easy, composed way she swung about as Lucia broke off their conversation at sight of Sally.

"Sally," Lucia beamed, "this is Jonni. Jonni Edwards. Jonni, this is my sister Sally."

Sally and Jonni said, "Hi."

Jonni's smile was shy, and her voice was quiet.

Lucia explained, "Her name is really Jonell. From Jon, her father. And Ellen, her mother."

Her eyes were black. Big and black. Sally thought uneasily that maybe Whit was right. Maybe Jonni was slick, after all.

Lucia said approvingly, "Jonni likes horses. She was looking at our barn, wondering if we still had space for a horse."

Jonni nodded. "I was hoping, when we moved out here, that I could have a horse. When the horse was stabled here, did you ride it?"

Lucia spoke first. "Sally was too little. And I wasn't even born yet when our sister Linda had Blazer—that was the horse's name."

Sally explained, "It was way back when there was prairie that way"—she pointed across the road—"as far as anyone could see. Now there are so many new subdivisions all around, and so many new houses, they had to build a new high school."

To this girl it probably didn't matter at all that they would be going to the new school. She might even think going to the new school would be better. There had been some girls and boys in school last term who'd been envious of those who could go to the new school.

Well, she wasn't one of them!

Lucia offered eagerly, "I'll show you where the old stall was, Jonni. And where the harness room was. And the water trough. And the feed."

Sally said, "Oh, she doesn't want to poke around in there—"

But even as Sally spoke, Jonni was saying, "I'd like that, Lu."

Just then Sally heard a voice, and this time there was no doubt that it was Sue's voice she heard.

Forgetting Jonni, she went racing toward the front walk.

"Sue!" she called out, just as Sue spotted her and cried, "Sally!"

They didn't kiss or hug or anything like that. They weren't the silly, sentimental type, Sally thought with a touch of pride. But she knew how Sue felt about her, and Sue certainly knew how she felt.

"You look simply great," Sue told her.

"And so do you," Sally returned the compliment. She smiled warmly.

Sue always sparkled. From kindergarten on, she had been one of the smallest girls in her class. This never kept her from being noticed. Not that she was actually noisy. But she said things that made people laugh. And she was always full of ideas—what to do, where to go, what to talk about.

All the way up to junior high, Sue had resisted having the snarls combed from her dark brown hair. Just as she had resisted scrubbing her freckled face. There were fewer freckles now—just enough, across the bridge of her perky nose, to accent the glowing cleanliness of her skin. And these days her hair was a shining tribute to a daily one hundred strokes of the hairbrush.

"I brought you something," Sally offered eagerly. "From California." They could go up to her room and get the present, and then talk and talk and talk. There was so much to talk about.

A boy's voice said, "What about me? What did you bring for me?"

It was Whit's voice. She started in surprise. He and Cornelius Cobb, who was called Corny, were sitting in Corny's car, an old convertible with a new white paint job. They had brought Sue over, she realized as she tried to think of a bright answer to Whit's question.

She could feel herself getting pink with embarrassment. "I guess I should have brought everybody some nice cool ocean breeze," she said at last, pretending to fan herself.

The boys laughed as if she'd said something original. Actually, during the past weeks she had heard many joking references to the ocean breeze, but she didn't think it necessary to mention this to Whit and Corny.

Encouraged by this minor success, she managed to relate a few of the high points of their vacation trip.

"Sounds great," Whit commented. Then he asked abruptly, "Where's the doll from down the street? Hasn't she been around?"

"Well, yes, she was," Sally answered, flustered again.

She looked over her shoulder toward where she had last seen Jonni, just in time to see Lucia mounting her bike. Even though it was a girl's bicycle, Lucia threw one leg across as if she were riding a boy's bike. Or as if she were mounting a horse.

Pedaling furiously, Lucia sang out, "Giddap, Horace!" as she flicked the rear end of the bicycle with a short leather whip.

Corny let out a whoop of laughter that ended in a shrill soprano because his voice was still changing. Sally was furious with him for laughing at her sister; at the same time she was furious with Lu for giving him cause to laugh at her, particularly in the presence of Whit.

Whit stared in exaggerated amazement. "What's with your kid sister? Has she flipped, or is she just a kook?"

"She's just playing," Sally managed to say, trying to say it lightly. "Her imagination works overtime. She likes to pretend. Somebody gave her the whip when we were out West."

In all the talk about Lu, the new girl was forgotten. Sally even forgot to tell Sue about Jonni, when the two of them finally went up to her bedroom to talk and talk and talk.

Most important talk of all, of course, was about Sally being forced to go to Hadley West, while Sue would still go to the old school.

"It's practically un-American," Sue declared. "It's as bad as the Communists. In a free country everybody should be able to choose the school she wants to go to."

Sally nodded in agreement. "There are some things in our system that need improving, I guess." Her heart was still heavy, but she felt comforted, having Sue there to share this mortal blow.

"And no matter where I am, or where you are," Sue declared, "nobody can keep us from being best friends."

Sally agreed. "Nothing can change that."

Sue fingered the small pin which she'd fastened to the lapel of her cotton blouse. This white enamel owl, with eyes of glowing orange, was Sally's homecoming gift to Sue, and she'd bought one just like it for herself.

Smiling impishly, Sue stated, "It's supposed to be

bad luck to give someone a pin—unless you also give a penny."

At that Sally laughed merrily and tumbled from the four-poster bed where they liked to sit cross-legged as they talked. She dug her coin purse from a still-unpacked suitcase.

"Here," she said, bringing forth a penny and placing it ceremoniously in Sue's outstretched hand. "Now our friendship is safe."

Momentarily solemn, Sue declared, "We'll be true friends forever."

"Forever," Sally agreed, choking back tears of joy at having a friend like Sue. It was almost worth being forced to go to the new school, to know how wonderfully loyal her best friend was.

From downstairs came the thump of the back screen door closing, followed by the clear call, "Sally! Sally! I need your help."

Sally sighed. "I'll have to help put the groceries away. And I suppose I'll have to dust and stuff. Mom will think of a million things for me to do."

"I know," Sue sympathized. "Your vacation is over."

They went downstairs arm-in-arm.

"Maybe you could stay for lunch," Sally suggested.

Mrs. Sorenson overheard this, and she called from the kitchen, "You are welcome to stay, Sue. But isn't that your brother waiting in the car out front?"

The two girls ran to check, and when they saw that Corny Cobb's repainted old convertible was back again, Sue hurried out to the curb.

Sally hung back a little, conscious that her eyes were probably red from all the emotion, and not wanting Whit to comment.

The boys were looking toward the house where the new neighbors had moved in. Sally saw what had caught their eye: A car was backing out of the driveway.

"Now that," Corny declared enviously, "is how a car should look."

This was also a convertible. It was also white. But beyond that there was little similarity between it and Corny's car.

"Yeah, man," Whit agreed. "And that's how a girl should look."

Driving the car was a woman with an elaborate blond hairdo. Seated next to her was a teen-aged girl, also blond. Both wore sleeveless white dresses and looked tanned.

Whit stood up, and Sally was not sure whether he

did it to allow Sue to sit between him and Corny, or to get an unobstructed view of the car down the street.

The blond girl caught sight of them and turned for a better look before the car headed in the other direction.

"Yeah, man," Whit said again. "That's what I call a car. And that's what I call a girl."

"And Lenore," Corny said. "That's what I call a name."

"Lenore?" Sally said uncertainly. "How do you know—"

Corny grinned. He was tall, he was dark, he was even rather handsome; but to Sally it had always seemed that Cornelius Cobb was just too sure of himself to be likable, and she wondered at Whit's friendship with him. Corny also had a reputation for being a little wild, but that, Sally thought, probably wasn't true, for after all he was Whit's closest friend.

"Why, honey chile," Corny drawled, "all the neighbors know her name. If you hadn't been on vacation—"

Whit spoke up impatiently. "Cut the corn pone act. Crank her up, Corny! Blast off! Maybe we can catch up to her."

Staring after Corny's convertible as its dual pipes

coughed smoke and something that sounded like a fender banged crazily as if it would surely shake loose, Sally wished the boys had waited just a little while, so she could be sure she'd understood what they were saying.

According to Corny, Lenore was the name of the girl who'd moved into the house two doors away.

But then what about Jonni? Where did she live?

From the house she heard her mother calling.

"Sally! I need your help."

"Coming," she answered automatically.

Moving slowly, reluctantly, toward the house, she pondered Whit's words: "Crank her up, Corny. Blast off! Maybe we can catch up to her."

Crank her up. "Her" meant Corny's car, of course. *Maybe we can catch up to her.* "Her," this time, probably didn't mean the other car. Or, if so, the reason was not to get a better view of the car. It was Lenore he wanted to see.

So that was why the boys had not only brought Sue over, but had come back for her. They had wanted to see Lenore.

Sally told herself she was in no hurry to meet Lenore. She was not at all sure that she was going to like this new girl. Not that it mattered. For she had Sue, and even though they would not be going to the same school, they would go right on being best friends. They had promised. Years ago they had promised. And today they had renewed that promise.

3

Dreaded Day

The day she had been dreading was here—the first day of the fall semester, both at Hadley East and Hadley West.

Sally came down to breakfast wearing her new knit outfit. She and Sue had decided that wearing it would be a kind of declaration of loyalty on Sally's part. A solid orange skirt. A solid orange cardigan. And under the cardigan, a sleeveless white sweater with diagonal orange stripes. For good measure, she had added her white enamel owl, the one like Sue's.

Her father's eyebrows rose at sight of her. "Very striking," he said. "But aren't you rushing the season?"

Lucia, wide-eyed with admiration, hastened to assure her father, "It's practically like fall. There's a nip to the breeze."

This adult-sounding weather report from his youngest daughter amused Mr. Sorenson, and he chuckled.

Mrs. Sorenson turned from the stove and the platter she was heaping with bacon and eggs to say, "I doubt if you'd be comfortable for long, Sally. The sun is sure to warm things up before the morning is far along."

"I don't expect to be in the sun," Sally pointed out. She'd be inside that horrid new school, that's where she'd be, and she needed the bright orange to aid her morale. Her white owl with the orange eyes wasn't enough. Not today.

As she placed the platter of soft-fried eggs and crisp bacon on the table, Mrs. Sorenson observed, "You might be a bit conspicuous, wearing the old school colors at the new school."

"I don't care," Sally insisted. But after saying it, she was not so sure. She didn't exactly want to be conspicuous. She didn't really want people staring at her.

Especially when tears were so close to the surface that she feared they might spill over at the slightest provocation.

She eyed her mother wonderingly. Her mother was always so calm. So efficient. Even at breakfast every hair went in the planned direction. She didn't try to hide the gray hairs that were crowding its former gingery color. She was slim and trim, and she ran the house in businesslike fashion. She had been a secretary after her graduation from college. For a while, before Linda was married, she had worked in the office of the grammar school Sally attended. Occasionally a pupil, looking impressed, would whisper, "Is that your mother, Sally?" She had always been proud to answer, "Yes."

Now she decided that her mother was probably right about the orange outfit. "I guess I'll wear it another day."

An approving smile was her reward.

All through breakfast Lucia chattered happily about school, concluding with a mild complaint: "I don't see why our school can't start at eight-thirty like yours does, Sally, instead of having to wait until nine."

That brought a rueful snort from Sally, as she wondered if she had ever been quite so impatient for school to start.

Changing to a dark blue cotton dress kept her thoughts busy for a little while. It was a pretty dress, and becoming to her, she knew. The white owl with his gleaming orange eyes was fastened where she was sure to see it and be comforted by it.

Although on any other day she might have been annoyed if Lu tagged after her, today she looked for her when she was ready to leave, wanting company part way—for of course she would not allow her sister to go all the way with her.

She asked her mother, "Do you know where Lu is?"

Mrs. Sorenson answered with a smile. "She's probably horseback riding. She took two apples—one for Horace, she said."

"Oh, really, Mother!"

She hoped Lu hadn't gone galloping off toward the new high school, as she'd done so often while it was under construction. One of these days, Sally decided, she would have to have a talk with her parents about Lucia. Imagination and make-believe were all right up to a point. But when people started making remarks—people like Whit, for instance. . . .

But she didn't want to think of Whit and all the others who were no doubt on their way right this minute to her dear old school.

She marched determinedly out of the house and headed toward Hadley West Township High School. A boy was crossing the street just ahead of her, and he slowed his long steps at sight of her.

"Hi, Sally," he greeted her cheerfully. "How was your long trip?"

"Fine, Myron," she answered. "What have you been doing all summer?"

It was a good question, she realized as soon as she'd spoken, for it should keep Myron busy while she continued to try to look and act calm and composed.

Myron Burdick lived down the block, on the opposite side of the street from the Sorensons. In junior high, when Sally and Sue were in seventh grade and Myron in eighth, he had suddenly become taller and taller, until he seemed to be all awkward bones without enough flesh to cover them properly. Last year he had sometimes walked to the school bus stop with the two girls, and it was then that Sue started referring to him as "the crane." It seemed an appropriate name for him; he was so long and leggy, and once the girls spied him with one leg actually dangling in midair, for all the world like a crane pausing at the water's edge.

"I was working," Myron said in answer to her question. "My uncle got me a job where he works, in a factory on the west side of the city."

This was an unexpected answer, and she exclaimed, "A factory! What kind of factory? What did you do?"

"I was in the shipping department. The firm sells musical instruments—cornets, trumpets, trombones, saxophones—and a couple of others. They don't make them; they assemble the parts and distribute the finished product."

Now it did not seem so strange that Myron had worked in a factory. For he liked music—not just the popular kind that she and her friends favored, but also classical music. And he had played a horn in the high school band last year.

She was about to ask if he hoped to play in the band this year, when her attention was diverted by a sound from the street alongside them. With a protesting shriek of brakes and tires, a car stopped abruptly. It was the now-familiar white convertible. At the wheel was the same woman with the elaborate hairdo. At her side was the blond girl, Lenore.

The two seemed to be consulting each other as they

looked in the direction of Sally and Myron. Then the car shot forward as abruptly as it had stopped, with the girl still looking toward them over her shoulder.

Sally had started to smile, determined to be polite to the new neighbors, even though there had been reports that the new people didn't want to have anything to do with anyone in the neighborhood. Her smile wavered uncertainly as the gleaming convertible streaked through traffic and was lost to her sight.

"Somebody," Myron said sharply, "had better tell Mrs. Andres we have speed laws out here, same as in the big city."

Sally found a kind of comfort in Myron's righteous wrath. She thought of Lenore and said, "She's pretty, isn't she?"

"Who? Oh, the new girl? I suppose so—if you like that type."

Apparently Whit liked Lenore's type, Sally thought, and then was glad that Myron had come along in time to walk with her. Boys and girls were converging from every direction. So many strangers. All hurrying into the new school building.

The old school was shaped as simply as a box. Additional red bricks had been added in the shape of extra boxes as enlargement became necessary. The new school was a lower, sprawling structure, with pale bricks interspersing vast expanses of glass. Inside the building, walls and ceilings of classrooms and corridors were painted in pleasant pastels. Sally had not yet seen the auditorium, but she knew it had been designed for the ultimate in utility, to function successfully not only for assemblies, plays, concerts, lectures, but for whatever need might arise.

The short while she'd been in the school on registration day had been taken up with the business of schedules and books and lockers and filling out information cards for the counselors. Today would be different. Today she would have to stay all day. Without so much as a glimpse of Sue.

As she went from one class to the next, she made mental notes of things to tell Sue when they got together after school. There were some familiar faces, and she tried to recall the names. There were even some teachers from the old school; and the principal, Mr. Hardie, had for some years been assistant principal at the original Hadley High.

Several times she caught a glimpse of Jonni Edwards, who had a ready smile, and she found a kind of comfort in noticing that Jonni looked much as she'd looked when they'd first met. Today Jonni wore a slim skirt with her blouse instead of jeans; her short dark hair was combed in simple lines, and Sally decided again that it was not a boyish cut. At lunchtime she looked about in the hope of persuading Jonni to sit with her in the cafeteria.

Gulping down soup and a sandwich, she pretended not to mind when it turned out that the girls around her were all freshmen. It wasn't that she looked down on freshmen; it was just that she felt obliged, as a sophomore, to pretend in the presence of these freshmen that she was perfectly at ease.

In her eagerness to get away she was making fast work of her favorite pie, lemon meringue, when everyone at the table stopped talking. All the girls were looking just beyond her left shoulder. Then someone spoke. Someone with a voice full of confidence.

"You weren't saving this seat for anyone, were you?"

It was Lenore, her blond hair appearing almost white above the deep brown of her straight-lined dress. Her skin wasn't really tanned, Sally decided. Or only a little, for it was naturally olive in color. Her eyes fascinated Sally. Not only were they a strange greenish-brown color, but she was almost certainly wearing eye makeup. Sally wondered if she could persuade her mother to let her use a little eye shadow, then decided it was probably useless even to ask, since it had taken all this while to get permission to wear lipstick—and not very much or very bright lipstick at that.

Recalling her manners, she said, "Oh, hello. I'm Sally Sorenson. We're neighbors on Maple Street."

"I know," Lenore answered, sinking into the next chair gracefully and rearranging the dishes on her tray. "I recognized you. That's why I wanted to sit here."

With everyone—not only at their table, but even some others around them—eyeing Lenore, Sally had the feeling of having become suddenly important. She hastened to introduce the freshmen girls to Lenore, glad that she had memorized all the names.

Lenore paid little attention to the others. She seemed eager to talk to Sally. "We were going to pick you up this morning. But we thought maybe you'd rather walk with that boy."

"Myron? Oh, he lives down our block. Sort of across from your house."

"He's not your boyfriend then?"

"Myron?" She laughed, because she would never have thought of Myron as a boyfriend.

Lenore laughed, too. "I really didn't see how he could be. He's so—" She shrugged her shoulders and wrinkled her nose in an amusing way.

"I know what you mean," Sally hastened to say. "Sue Fowler—she's my best friend—you'll be meeting her one of these days"—Sally leaned closer so that nobody but Lenore would hear—"Sue calls Myron 'the crane.' "

"One of those long-legged— Oh, that's a scream!" Lenore declared.

For just a moment Sally had a guilty feeling, as if she'd betrayed Myron in telling this about him. But when Lenore burst into laughter, she joined in.

They tried to smother their laughter, but the harder they tried, the harder it became. All afternoon, the mere sight of each other in the corridors brought on fits of giggles.

Sally could scarcely wait to tell Sue about this, as well as about all the rest of the events of the day. In her last class that afternoon she spied Jonni sitting in the row behind her.

When the dismissal bell rang, Jonni hurried toward her.

"I was so glad to see you today," Jonni said. "I hardly know anyone yet, and it seemed a little easier, seeing a girl I recognized."

"I know," Sally agreed, remembering her first day in junior high, and her first day as a high school freshman, and how important it had been to know that Sue was there somewhere among all those strangers.

Their lockers were not far apart, Sally and Jonni discovered, and after putting some things in and taking other things out of their lockers, they walked from the school building together.

Jonni wasn't exciting to be with, like Lenore. And she certainly wasn't like Sue. But she was nice, Sally decided, though now she was not so certain that Jonni had a kind of flair. Had she only imagined this because she'd supposed Jonni was the slick girl Whit had raved about?

"We live not very far from here," Jonni told Sally, with a sweep of her arm in the direction opposite from the Sorenson home. "Could you come over?"

As Sally hesitated, Jonnie urged, "For a little while? My mother isn't home. She's working at the store today."

Sally almost said, "Oh, you live in the crackerbox subdivision?"

There had been so much talk, as well as stories in the local paper and letters to the editor, about one area among the many areas that had built up so quickly around the town of Linden. Zoning laws had not been specific enough to halt the construction of several streets of "shell houses." Some of the residents of Linden resented having what they called the crackerbox subdivision so close to their own more substantial homes.

Sally was glad she had not blurted this out. Instead she said politely, "Thanks, but I can't."

The disappointment in Jonni's eyes prompted her to add, "Maybe another day. But there is something I have to do today."

She had to see Sue, that was what she had to do, she told herself as she hurried home. Sue, after hearing about Jonni's interest in the Sorenson barn, had called her "the horse girl." It did not seem quite as funny now as it had when Sue had said it. And she wondered uneasily if perhaps she should have gone with Jonni. She could have, for a little while. As it was, she'd have to wait for Sue's bus.

She could understand that it wouldn't be any fun to go home to an empty house, with no friends waiting or anything. Maybe tomorrow she would invite

Jonni to go home with her, to meet Sue.

Her mother had been right about the weather. The sun was hot, and when she dropped off her books at home she changed into denim pedal pushers and a sleeveless blouse.

Munching on an apple and molasses cookies, she hurried two blocks east and a half block north, to Sue's house.

Mrs. Fowler was puttering in her flower border at the side of the house. She looked up to ask, "How was your first day in the new school, Sally?"

"Awful," Sally answered with a wry grin.

Mrs. Fowler smiled indulgently. She was a plump little woman, always cheerful, and Sally was very fond of her.

"When you are my age," Mrs. Fowler declared, "you will look back and think this was the most carefree time of your life."

Sally doubted that. She doubted it very much. In fact, she was sure Mrs. Fowler had forgotten what it had been like to be fifteen. But perhaps this was understandable. After all, it had been a long while since Mrs. Fowler was fifteen.

Impatient to see and talk with Sue, Sally decided to wait for her at the bus corner. When the last school bus had come and gone and no Sue, she walked slowly home.

She tried to keep her mind on her homework, to get the day's assignments out of the way so there would be plenty of time for talking to Sue. Mrs. Fowler had assured her that she would tell Sue to call. Mrs. Fowler must have forgotten, Sally decided, and when it was almost supper time she dialed Sue's number.

Sue was home. Her voice was all bubbly with excitement, the way Sally had heard it so many times.

"I was going to call you," Sue said, not at all apologetic. "But Whit and I kept talking about Ann Ainsley."

"Who?"

"Ann Ainsley. She lives in Robinswood, Sally, and she asked me and Ruth McGowen to ride home with her."

Robinswood was another of the housing areas that had made a new high school a necessity. Robinswood was the most exclusive, and was situated among tall trees along Robins Creek.

Sally wanted to know more about Ann Ainsley. "You mean she drives?" That would make her older than the two girls.

"No, her brother drove us. He's a senior. Isn't that a coincidence, Sally? She has a brother who is a senior. And I have a brother who is a senior. And Ann and I are sophomores. Isn't that a coincidence?"

Sally agreed that this was a coincidence.

"Poor Whit!" Sue said. "He practically flipped when he saw Lester's car. Les is Ann's brother. His car is really dreamy, Sally. And you know what Whit is always saying about a set of wheels!"

Yes, she knew. Whit was always saying: "I've just got to get me a set of wheels."

Whit had had a car. Not much of a car. Not even as much of a car as Corny Cobbs' battered convertible. But it had been his, bought with money from his bank account, money earned and money given him for Christmas and other special occasions.

Whit had been caught speeding, which was bad enough. Then he lost control of the car going around a corner and rammed a light post. He insisted the fault this time was with the car. But even before the police magistrate forbade Whit to drive for a whole year, Mr. Fowler had decreed the car was to be sold. The year was up, but Mr. Fowler had not yet given permission for another car.

Sue was raving on. "You should see their house,

Sally. You can see all outdoors through glass walls. . . ."

Sally scarcely heard the description of the house in the woods. She had thought she had things of interest to share with Sue. Now she felt all deflated. Like a balloon after a pin had been stuck in it.

She realized that Sue was waiting for her to answer.

Sue said, giggling a little as she repeated her question, "I suppose the horse girl was among those present at Hadley West today?"

There was no point in mentioning that Jonni had asked her to her home. Sue would just make a funny remark about the crackerbox subdivision, if she learned that this was where Jonni lived.

But she could mention Lenore.

"Oh," she said, "Lenore and I had the most fun at lunch—"

Sue interrupted with a squeal. "Lenore? The white convertible girl?"

Sally tried to sound casual about it all as she said, "Lenore wanted me to ride in the white convertible to school this morning. I guess maybe tomorrow I will."

Lenore had not mentioned anything about a ride

tomorrow, Sue thought guiltily to herself.

But she had to have something to tell Sue. And more than likely it was the truth, even though she hadn't been asked yet.

4

The Little Monsters

For just a little while, eating her dinner, Sally almost forgot how put out she was with Sue for going to Robinswood after school. Her mother's Swedish meat balls and corn on the cob never had tasted quite so good. As for the peach cobbler, warm from the oven and drenched with cream, she just couldn't imagine anything more delicious.

After a second helping of cobbler her mother spoiled her appetite by saying, "We might as well get back into harness. Sally, tonight you wash the dishes."

She let out a moan of protest, though she knew it would do her no good. Getting "back into harness" called for her both to wash and dry the dishes. When it was Lucia's turn, Lu dried and their mother washed. At the moment this seemed a most unfair arrangement, though before going on vacation it had seemed better than having Lu as her helper. They had all been happier after agreeing to this arrangement.

As her chore for the time being, Lucia took the kitchen wastebasket out and emptied it into a trash burner at the back of the yard. Then she was off on her bicycle, calling out, "Giddap, Horace! Good boy, Horace!" She raised her new whip in a mighty arc, only to bring it down with a gentle flick where the right rear end of a horse would be if she were actually riding a horse.

Watching all this through the kitchen window, Sally said in mild exasperation, "Mother, don't you think you should speak to Lu about Horace?"

"I have," her mother said in her calm way. "She has strict orders to put her bicycle away well before dark, and I reminded her of it again today."

This was not what Sally meant, and she was about to say so when her father, who had gone to answer the telephone in the den, returned to the kitchen to say, "The Stantons want to hear about the trip, Alice; they asked us to drop in for a little while. Sally can hold the fort here, can't you, Sally?"

"Of course I can. I'm not a child," she reminded him.

"Just be sure Lu puts her bike away," her mother reminded her.

When the station wagon backed out of the garage and carried her parents on their way to visit with their friends, the Stantons, Sally dawdled over finishing the dishes. She was in no hurry to do her school assignments. She wished Sue would phone again. By this time Sue should have realized that she hadn't been very nice this afternoon, keeping her waiting and everything. It was almost as if Sue had forgotten already that they were best friends. Though of course that was not possible. But just the same Sue might have been more considerate, Sally told herself with mounting resentment.

She was scouring the black iron skillet in which her mother had browned the meat balls, when she heard running footsteps across the back porch. Lucia, who was not given to crying, was in tears. The rubber band was missing from one of her pigtails, setting the hair on that side of her head flying as she ran into the house. She stopped when she saw Sally.

Sally dropped the skillet, causing dishwater to splash the front of her blouse and pedal pushers and onto the kitchen linoleum.

"What's the matter? What happened? Are you hurt?" Sally asked, her annoyance forgotten.

Lucia was using her knuckles to mop away her tears. Reaching for a box of tissues, Sally dabbed with one wad of tissues at Lucia's eyes while she offered another wad for Lucia's nose.

"Did you fall off your bike?" she asked with concern, looking for cuts or bruises.

"It was those horrid Andres boys," Lucia answered at last.

"Lenore's brothers? What did they do?"

Lucia blew her nose. "They blocked the sidewalk." She gulped down a sob. "They pulled the rubber band off my hair." She clutched at the loosening strands that were kinked from constant braiding. "They wouldn't let me past!"

"Well, of all the— Did they give any reason?"

"Because I called one Roy. His name is Royal. The other one, Junior, said what did I mean by calling his brother Roy! And then Royal said, 'Yeah, what do you mean by calling me that?' And they wouldn't let me past!" Lucia sniffed as if she were about to cry again.

"Of all the pests! They need someone to tell them off, if you ask me." Sally marched to the door, eager to do battle with these boys who had tormented her little sister.

The boys were standing on the sidewalk in front of their home. One was younger than Lucia, the other slightly older, but they were about the same height. Both were overweight. They looked alike, but not at all like their sister Lenore. Both had pale eyes, and brown hair cut close to the scalp. They stood with hands in the pockets of stiff new levis, and with their chins thrust forward as Sally approached them.

"Why," she demanded without preliminaries, "did you push Lucia and pull her hair and keep her from riding her bike?"

Neither answered, and she asked again with rising fury, "Why did you push my sister?"

At that one boy said with exaggerated surprise, "Oh, is she your sister?"

The other said insolently, "It's our sidewalk. I guess we can stop anybody on our sidewalk."

She managed to speak with reasonable calm. "This

is a public sidewalk, and anyone has the right to use it."

At that, one boy laughed scornfully. "Har-dee-har, har, har!"

The other shouted gleefully, "Ho-dee-ho, ho, ho!"

She wanted to slap them. She wanted to knock their heads together. She had never before been so furious with anyone. While she stood, trying to restrain her anger, she heard Lenore's voice.

Lenore, looking pleased to see her, came from the house to say, "I looked for you after school."

Sally forced her lips into a stiff smile. "I looked for you, too."

"I'm glad you came over. Come on in," Lenore invited.

"Well—I came over to talk to your brothers. My sister came home crying. They pulled her hair and—"

Lenore whirled on her brothers. "So you've been picking on a girl now—two boys against one girl! Aren't you proud of yourselves? Little monsters, that's what you are! Pulling a girl's hair! It takes brains to do a thing like that, doesn't it? Junior! Royal! Big shots, that's what you are—not!"

The one called Junior said lamely, "Well, she had a whip in her hand."

The one named Royal said, "Sure, she had a whip."

Lenore said, "A likely story!"

Sally felt honor-bound to say that Lucia actually had a whip. "But she wouldn't even hit Horace with—" She stopped in confusion.

Just then Mrs. Andres came from the house, saving Sally from the need to explain about Horace. She felt grateful to this tall, slender woman with the elaborate hairdo who was wearing Capri pants and a matching blouse as pale as her hair.

Soon Mrs. Andres was scolding the boys, scolding so shrilly that Sally began to feel embarrassed, and she wished she had stayed at home.

The boys no longer looked cocky. They hung their heads, and Royal said, "Aw, we were only kidding."

"Then see to it that you cut out that kind of kidding," Mrs. Andres ordered sharply.

She turned to Sally with a smile. "Come in and see our house."

"Oh—thanks, but I should get home."

The woman was insistent. "It won't take long. Come see what we've done to the house."

So Sally went into the house that at one time had been much like theirs. She all but gasped at sight of the elaborate furnishings. Obviously Mrs. Andres liked white and pastels, for even the carpeting was pale as foam. Most of the upholstery was sea green or in shades of blue, with occasional touches of black. Exposed wood surfaces were either white or black. Furniture curved to fit corners. It all looked as if it might have been transplanted directly from a store window.

Mrs. Andres looked pleased when Sally exclaimed, "It's all so glamorous! It makes your house look entirely different from ours."

Lenore said at once, "Oh, I'd like to see how your house looks, Sally."

Mrs. Andres laughed. "Nothing like inviting yourself, Lenore."

"Oh, that's all right," Sally insisted. "I'll be glad to have Lenore come over."

But she wished it could have been another time. She hadn't finished the dishes. And, though her mother was such a good housekeeper, her parents had left in a hurry and there had been no time for "picking up."

She took Lenore in the front way. Just as she had expected, there were newspapers everywhere. Not only the evening paper, but part of the morning one. The comics were on the floor where Lucia had been reading them. Her mother had been studying clothing ads while her father, as usual, had thoroughly examined the financial and political news.

Viewing the house as she was sure Lenore was seeing it, everything looked horribly shabby. And instead of fancy decorator touches such as she had seen at the Andres', there were all the sentimental knickknacks. Things she and Lucia—and even Linda years ago—had given their parents for Christmas or birthdays. She hesitated to show Lenore the kitchen, not only because of the dishes she hadn't finished putting away, but because of the potholders and hot pads and other things from as far back as their kindergarten days that her mother kept on display. It had never occured to her to mind before. Until today she had considered it natural to keep all these things.

Lenore kept saying, "Oh, how nice!" or, "What a nice cozy house!" as if she really meant it.

Sally led the way upstairs. "This is my room. Some of the things belonged to my great-grandmother." She had always been so proud of the four-poster. At the moment she had no enthusiasm even for the new canopy, patterned in pink roses to match the ruffles on her dressing table. As for the dresser, no amount of rubbing could remove the streaks from the mirror.

Lenore looked startled. "You really mean it? All this stuff was from your ancestors?"

"It really was," Sally said, even as she saw that Lenore's glance rested on her small drop-front desk near the window. This had come from a secondhand store, a fact which had never affected her affection for the desk. But at the moment she did not want to be put in the position of having to explain about the desk.

So she hurried her guest down the stairs. She had hoped to avoid the kitchen, but Lucia called to them, "Come see what I've got for you."

Lenore greeted Lucia with an apology. "I'm sorry about those little monsters—those brothers of mine, Lucia. I hope they didn't hurt you?"

Lucia had washed away the traces of tears. Both her braids were again confined by rubber bands, one less smoothly than the other. She had poured lemonade, prepared earlier by her mother, into three glasses, and she had piled cookies onto a paper plate. She had even put a container of paper napkins on the kitchen table. And she had pulled up three chairs.

"Oh, I'm all right," she assured Lenore with a wide smile. "Have some lemonade. I poured it for you."

She looked so proud of herself. And Sally was proud

of her, of course. But she wished Lu had thought to remove the washed and dried dishes heaped on the table. And the big black skillet was still in the dishpan. The Andres had an electric dishwasher. If they had an electric dishwasher she wouldn't have left a splash of water on the floor.

That reminded Sally that her blouse and pedal pushers had been splashed when she dropped the skillet. She certainly didn't look all crisp and clean, the way Lenore looked.

She felt more than a little embarrassed as she tried to get the dishes out of the way in a hurry. Lenore sat back, cool and calm, sipping her lemonade and nibbling on a cooky. She apologized again to Lucia for what her brothers had done, and Lucia responded by urging her to have another cooky and more lemonade.

At last Lenore said, "I suppose I'd better get home."

"I suppose," Sally said, getting to her feet, "you want to do your homework."

"Homework? Oh, for school. There wasn't much. Maybe I'll leave it for homeroom tomorrow."

The two girls walked out to the front porch.

Lenore suggested, "Let's walk to school together tomorrow."

"Yes, let's," Sally agreed eagerly.

"I'm glad everything worked out all right with your sister."

"Yes. But sometimes," Sally confided, "Lu's imagination gets the best of her. She even has wild ideas that something strange is going on in the carriage house. That's what she calls your garage—she calls it the carriage house."

Lenore's expression changed abruptly. "What are you talking about?"

"Oh—I told you. Lu imagines things."

"What kind of things?" Lenore wanted to know.

She didn't want to mention Horace. "Oh—made-up things."

When Lenore continued to stare at her, frowning, Sally said, "Kids can be little monsters, you know."

At that, Lenore smiled a little. "They sure can! See you in the morning, Sally."

"See you in the morning, Lenore."

She was pleased at the prospect of walking to school with Lenore, this girl who was so unlike any girl she had ever known.

But she was annoyed with Lucia, and she decided again that she must speak to her parents about Lu and her silly imaginings.

5

Just a Little Nothing

If you did something over and over enough times it began to seem natural, Sally decided, not altogether happy over this discovery. Already it seemed natural to go to school with Lenore each morning, though she would certainly have preferred going with Sue. And it no longer seemed strange to go to the new school, though of course her affections were still with the old school.

Whenever the weather was bad Mrs. Andres drove them. It was exciting to have girls and boys along the way turn and look at the white convertible enviously, and it made her feel important when someone mentioned having seen her in it.

Myron Burdick sometimes joined them. At sight of him Lenore would whisper, "Lo and behold, the crane approaches."

Often Sally had difficulty in smothering her giggles, especially when Lenore continued to whisper remarks such as "He walks! He talks! Can he be human?"

There were times, though, when she was uncomfortable for fear Myron would overhear, and she wished he would find someone else to walk to school with.

One day she and Myron got into a mild argument over school athletic contests. Afterward she could not remember what started it all. But there she was, declaring, "Of course a boy should go out for a school team if he's able."

She certainly didn't mean that Myron should try out for a team. For that matter, she certainly didn't believe that any boy should try out for a team at Hadley West. For she certainly didn't care one little speck about any Hadley West team.

Myron protested, "But don't you think a guy should be free to decide for himself how he wants to spend his free time? Maybe he figures he'd be better off doing something else—"

"Like playing in the band," Lenore interjected, and to Sally she whispered, "Where he won't get hurt."

Myron asserted, "Well, sure, the band if that's what he's interested in. Everyone doesn't have to be interested in the same things, for cat's sake!"

A few mornings later it was raining and Mrs. Andres drove them to school. This time Lenore did not whisper her comment about Myron's long legs: "They should make foldaway contraptions to get legs like those into a car."

Sally noted the color of embarrassment that tinged Myron's cheeks and ears. She hastened to point out, "Long legs are an advantage sometimes. For basketball players, for instance."

That reminded Lenore. "I see you tossing basketballs into the ring on your garage with that little creep that lives next door to you, Myron."

Looking even more embarrassed, Myron admitted, "I baby-sit with Harold sometimes. Practicing free throws is one way of keeping him amused."

Lenore shrieked, "Baby-sit! You baby-sit?"

Myron said gravely, "Employment opportunities

for a man my age are limited in Linden."

"But baby-sit—with that little creep?"

"Oh, he's a good kid," Myron insisted. "He's sort of different, that's all. His mother works part-time, and she needs somebody to—"

Again Lenore interrupted him. "Junior and Royal say he's a creep," she declared, as if this settled the question.

Sally waited for Mrs. Andres to make a comment, but Mrs. Andres merely smiled. She was sure her mother would have said something if she had been in Mrs. Andres' place, though just what she would have said, Sally wasn't sure.

By lunchtime she had forgotten her feeling of being annoyed with Lenore. Having lunch with Lenore was fun. Sometimes she poked fun at the teachers, or her classmates. Sally noticed the growing number of girls who tried to sit close to them so that they could laugh at Lenore's remarks.

The first week of school, Sally tried to save a place for Jonni. She gave this up when she saw that Lenore didn't take to Jonni. As for Jonni, she was not the kind to push her way where she was not wanted. This very fact made Sally feel guilty sometimes.

After a while she noticed that if she stopped in the

halls to say a few words to Jonni, a boy lingered nearby, always the same boy, and so she no longer felt that she had left Jonni all to herself.

Boys were always eyeing Lenore, poking each other and nodding toward her. Sometimes one would whistle. Sally wished she were allowed to wear eye makeup, as Lenore did, and use expensive-smelling perfume, and have her hair done at the beauty parlor. Or if she had Lenore's wardrobe, maybe the boys would whistle at her. But probably not, she decided dolefully. She just wasn't the glamour type. But the right clothes would surely help.

She was not the only one who envied Lenore's smart sweaters and skirts and blouses and dresses. The girls who were fortunate enough to sit at their table usually made flattering comments. Lenore always looked pleased, and she thanked them. But she never invited any of them to her home, or made any real effort to be friends with anyone but Sally.

During the week Sally seldom saw Sue. They talked over the phone, but now that they were together so seldom, they seemed to find less to talk about. On several Saturdays they spent part of the day together, and there were moments when it almost seemed as if things were the same between them as ever. On Sundays they saw each other at church and managed to find time to talk afterward.

Football season brought on a crisis. The girls had agreed, when first they learned that Sally would be going to the new school, that they would go together to all home games at the old school. Nothing had been said about games not played at home. The first game of the season Hadley East was scheduled to play Baker, a high school about five miles away and Hadley's traditional rival. As the day for the big game neared, Sally waited impatiently for Sue to mention the all-important Baker game. For of course Sue would be going. And surely they would go together? She wanted to talk about tickets and transportation and what to wear and all the other important details of going to a football game.

By Wednesday she was so keyed up she could scarcely sit still. Her mother said, "The sensible thing would be to come right out and tell Sue you've been counting on going to the game with her, Sally. It could be that she is taking it for granted that you prefer to go to your own school game."

"She couldn't possibly think that!" Sally insisted. "Sue knows how I feel!"

But if Sue knew how she felt, she would surely

have said something by now, Sally thought miserably.

On Thursday, after waiting and waiting for Sue to telephone, she lifted the receiver and dialed Sue's number. She had to know, one way or another.

Sue was home. In a way she almost wished she hadn't been. But now that she'd got this far, she had to ask.

"I suppose you are going to the game Saturday?"

Sue, who was usually so quick with answers, was just a little slow this time. "Why, Sally, I must have told you. Ann Ainsley's brother offered to drive us over to Baker, to the game."

For just a moment her heart bounded upward. "Offered to drive us," Sue had said. For just a moment Sally thought "us" included her. But Ann Ainsley's brother wouldn't be driving her. Lester—that was the name of the brother of the girl Sue was always talking about. The girl from Robinswood. The girl from the exclusive subdivision. The girl whose brother had a car that Whit was "really rocked" about, according to Sue.

She tried to be fair, in her thoughts, to Sue. For she was not certain that they had made any plans to go to the Baker game together. Maybe she had just taken this for granted all the time.

Her heart was painfully heavy as she said, "I hope you have a good time."

"Well, thanks, old pal." Relief was plainly to be heard in Sue's words. "And I hope you have fun. Are you and Lenore going to your game?"

"No. Lenore doesn't care much about things like that."

As for herself, Sue should know that she was not interested in any games at Hadley West.

When Sue did not comment, Sally said, "Maybe Lenore and I will go shopping." She had almost forgotten that Lenore had suggested a shopping trip for Saturday. She had had no real desire to go. Lenore would be doing all the buying.

Sue seemed to find their proposed shopping trip exciting. "Will you go to the new shopping center?"

"I think so," Sally answered, only to realize that this was what Lenore had suggested. "Lenore said she'd cancel her beauty parlor appointment, or change it to another time, if I'd go shopping with her."

"She did?" Sue sounded impressed. Then, with a laugh, she said, "What Whit wouldn't give if the white convertible girl would treat him like that! He and the other boys are always making remarks about

Lenore and her convertible."

Sally was not exactly happy to hear that Whit was always making remarks about Lenore. But maybe this meant that he was not seriously interested in Ann Ainsley. She found some comfort in that thought.

Lenore was pleased to hear that Sally had decided to go with her on Saturday, after all. Her mother was going somewhere with her father, she said. "But Weejee will drive us. I can always get Weejee to drive us."

The young man called Weejee worked for Mr. Andres. Just what kind of work he did, Sally did not know, but he went in and out of the carriage house at all hours, according to Lucia.

The three of them sat in the front seat of the convertible. Weejee, as usual, had on dark sunglasses. A sleeveless white sweater was pulled down to the hips of his silky-looking slacks. He scarcely spoke as the car rolled swiftly along one of the new expressways in the area, but the quick movement of his head toward Lenore whenever she spoke made Sally uncomfortable. She was sure Lenore was aware of his glances, though she talked exclusively to Sally and did not once turn her head toward Weejee.

"Wait here," Lenore ordered peremptorily when

Weejee brought the car to a smooth stop close to one of the fashionable stores in the new shopping center.

Sally started to get out of the car, but Lenore held her back as she addressed Weejee. "When I said wait here I didn't mean you can't get out and open the door for us—like a gentleman."

Weejee laughed heartily. "If you'd of told me, I'd of wore my chauffeur's uniform."

He lifted a lazy hand toward the door handle on his side of the car, but Lenore reached angrily across Sally to open the door on their side. "Come on, Sally. Let's get out of here."

They could hear Weejee, still laughing, as they walked past miniature trees and planters of bright geraniums, and into the deep carpeting of the Flair Shop.

This was a new shopping experience for Sally. Lenore did not once ask the cost of anything or look at a price tag.

"I want a mohair sweater," she told the saleswoman.

There was no pawing through things on a counter. Sweaters were brought to Lenore, sweaters in every luscious shade imaginable. Finally she chose one in a color called lemon peel.

"You want one, too, don't you, Sally?"

Sally said she had not come to buy a sweater.

"We could have twin sweaters," Lenore suggested eagerly.

Sally hedged. "That color is good for you, but maybe not for me."

"Then why don't you take the strawberry pink?"

With the clerk listening, Sally could not bring herself to admit that she didn't have either a charge account or the cash to pay for something like this. Instead she said, "I have a knitted outfit I haven't even worn." It was a fact. Her orange and white. The old school colors.

Lenore seemed to understand that. "I know. My mother chews me out sometimes and says I can't buy something because I haven't worn what I have. But I'll buy one for you.Then your mother can't squawk."

She started to give the order to the clerk, but Sally was firm. This she knew she must not do. Her mother would not allow her to accept such a gift, that she knew.

Finally Lenore conceded with a shrug, "You win."

In the flurry of finishing her shopping, she seemed to have forgotten about the sweater she had wanted Sally to have.

But when they reached home Lenore handed Sally

a small package. "You can accept this, I'm sure. It's just a little nothing."

The "little nothing" was the bottle of perfume that had been Lenore's last purchase, a new brand called Forever Faithful.

"Oh— How sweet of you, Lenore. But I enjoyed myself—that was enough—I don't need a gift!"

She took it, at Lenore's insistence. She took it into the house and showed the lovely flacon to her mother.

Mrs. Sorenson said at once, "I'm sorry, Sally, but you must return it to Lenore."

"But she'll be hurt," Sally said. "She really wanted to buy me a mohair sweater. This is just a little—"

Her mother interrupted. "If she'd given you bubble bath, or even cologne, that would be different. But this new perfume has been well advertised lately. The price is thirty dollars an ounce. This is a one-ounce bottle."

Sally stared at the daintily shaped container. Lenore had charged everything. Mr. Andres must make lots of money if they could afford to let Lenore spend money this way. Or was it possible that Lenore had made a mistake and didn't realize how much this new perfume cost?

"I'll take it back to her," Sally agreed.

She was glad Weejee was not in sight, and that it was Lenore who answered the door.

At first Lenore looked puzzled as to why Sally was returning her gift. "Don't you like it?"

Then she said lightly, "I'll give it to my mother. Yes, that's a good idea. She's been screaming at me for helping myself to her perfume. I'll give her this and maybe it will get her off my back."

Sally walked slowly home. She didn't know what to make of Lenore. Nor of Lenore's mother if, as Lenore seemed so sure, Mrs. Andres would be pleased to get the perfume.

Sometimes her own mother seemed too strict. But she didn't know what to think of Lenore's mother. Or of Lenore.

6

The Big Game

"Sally," Lucia yelled up the staircase, "Sue is here."

She had started her homework as soon as she got home from school, just because there was nothing better to do. Pushing the books and pen and paper into a heap on her desk, she ran to the hallway, calling, "Come on up, Sue!"

It was just like old times. They sat on Sally's bed and talked and talked and talked, and laughed and laughed.

Sue said, "I wish you could have been with us at

the Baker game. I missed you."

That took away all the hurt. It didn't matter so much that she hadn't gone. What mattered was that Sue had wished she were there.

It was also important that her old school had won.

"Whit says we're sure to win the championship this year," Sue exulted. "After beating Baker twenty-seven to six, Whit says the other teams in the conference will be pushovers."

Beating Hadley's old rival was important. It didn't matter to Sally that the school she now attended had lost its game. "But I don't understand," she admitted, "why Hadley West doesn't get to play Hadley East."

"But we do play against each other," Sue said.

"I know, but it's not a conference game. That's what I don't understand."

Sue admitted, "I don't really understand that, either, about why we aren't in the same conference."

Even sharing their ignorance was pleasant. They talked of other things, and then the talk returned to football.

"Conference game or not," Sue declared, "the game between the new and old Hadley will be the big game of the season. And our school will slaughter yours, of course. Everyone says so."

Sally felt slightly resentful at having Sue dismiss the new school's chances so lightly. "After all," she pointed out, "they're starting from scratch. They've been trying to work up school spirit, I guess. Anyway, they've asked for school cheers, and songs too, I think. I wasn't paying much attention."

"Why don't you write a song for them?" Sue suggested jokingly.

Sally pretended to take this seriously, and after a while she announced, "I have it. How's this for a school song?"

She stood up, the better to recite solemnly:

"Hadley West!
Hadley West!
We'll be true and
Do our best!"

"Oh, that's a riot!" Sue squealed. "You must turn it in, Sally. You must! It's a riot!"

While Sue was there she wrote the words carefully on a sheet of paper. "I'll turn it in," she promised. "But I'm not signing my name to it."

She walked home with Sue, and they talked some more about the "big game," the game when the two Hadley schools would compete against each other.

"I'll wear my orange and white knit to the game," Sally planned aloud, "to let everyone know which team I'm pulling for."

"Neat!" Sue applauded. "And you can sit on our side of the field. Then nobody will have any doubt about your loyalty."

They laughed some more. Being with Sue was such fun. Walking back home, Sally was sure nobody had ever had a better friend. She and Sue. They might be parted during school hours, but nobody and nothing could keep them from being best friends forever. She would be understanding when Sue became involved with goings-on at the old school. After all, she couldn't expect a lively girl like Sue not to make new friends or not to get involved in whatever was going on at her school. But that couldn't change their friendship.

It seemed forever before the Hadley East-Hadley West game. In the meantime Hadley East kept on winning games, and Hadley West went on losing.

When the old school played its homecoming game, Sally waited for Sue to say something about getting a ticket for her. But all Sue mentioned, on the rare occasions when she found a few moments to spare, was the parade. Sue was on the parade committee, and she was determined that it was to be the best homecoming parade the school had ever known.

Sue did say, "You must be sure to see the parade, Sally."

But Sue did not offer to get a ticket for Sally for the homecoming game.

How different things would be if she were still going to the old school! She would be taking part in all this fun and excitement along with Sue. And they would be double-dating at parties and dances. As it was, she had no desire to go to any affairs at the new school.

Sue would not forget their plans for the old school-new school game, Sally told herself consolingly.

And Sue did not forget. She telephoned to explain why it had seemed necessary to change the plans.

"The gang is going together," Sue explained contritely. "It's Ann Ainsley's birthday, so all of us are sitting together and going to her house afterward for birthday cake. I'm sorry things didn't work out the way we planned, Sally. But you know how it is with birthdays. You don't mind, do you?"

"Oh, of course not," she lied.

She wanted to weep with disappointment. She wanted to cry out, "That darned Ann Ainsley! Why can't she ask someone else instead of you, Sue?"

She didn't say it, of course. Not even to Lenore, when Lenore came over to say that she would be going into the city with her mother on the day of the game.

"I wouldn't go to the game anyway. School games are kid stuff." Lenore scoffed. "All that school loyalty jazz! School games are for kids, and for people who go to the games to cash in on their bets."

Sally was shocked. Surely Lenore couldn't be serious? Sometimes she just wasn't sure whether Lenore was joking. She just didn't know what to say when Lenore said things like that.

She went to the game, but she didn't wear her orange and white outfit. She might not have gone at all if it hadn't been for Jonni. They almost bumped into each other near their lockers on Friday.

"Are you going to the game tomorrow?" Jonni asked in her forthright way.

"I don't know," Sally answered. "Are you?"

Jonni repeated Sally's words: "I don't know. Are you?"

They laughed a little at that, and decided to go together.

There was something about Jonni, Sally decided.

Something that made her feel steadier, more sure of herself.

She was glad she had decided to go when she and Jonni met at the entrance to the athletic field. It no longer seemed so important that Hadley West had not won a single game, while Hadley East had won all but one and could very well win the championship if they won their last conference game, to be played the following week. What mattered today was that the weather was perfect, the grandstands were already almost overflowing, and everyone was as filled with excitement as if this were the championship game instead of the first athletic contest between the old and the new schools.

Sally envied the cheerleaders their jobs. She had hoped, before she knew that she would be changing schools, to try out as a cheerleader in her sophomore year.

"Aren't their outfits darling?" She sighed, eyeing the brief ruffled skirts and waist-length turtle-necked sweaters in the school colors, maroon and beige.

At the end of the first quarter the score was tied, seven to seven, and the cheerleaders for each school led calls for touchdowns. Sally was wishing she had attended the pep rally so that she might be familiar with the school cheers. By the end of the half, the score was again tied, thirteen to thirteen. Stirring music from the school bands added to the crowd's enthusiasm.

A boy sitting behind them kept talking to Jonni, and during the intermission Jonni introduced him to Sally. This was the boy she had noticed near Jonni a number of times. His name, she learned, was Judd Clemens. He was not very tall, but he was husky, with broad shoulders. His chin was square-cut, and he had a twinkle in his eyes.

"I'm one of the Crackerbox Kids," Judd said cheerfully.

Sally had heard rumors of trouble between two groups of boys in school: those who had attended the old school and resented having to change schools, and newcomers from the so-called crackerbox subdivision.

Judd seemed very likable. Sally welcomed the bits of information he offered that made the game more understandable to her.

All along she had expected her old school to win. Yet when they scored two touchdowns in the third quarter she was not entirely happy at what seemed a sure victory.

The girls in maroon and beige went running out

onto their side of the field to lead another rallying cry:

"Hadley West!
Hadley West!"

Hadley West students responded with a mighty shout:

"Yea, team!
Rah! Rah! Rah!"

The cheerleaders sang out:

"We know you
Will do your best!"

Again the stands rocked to the mighty cry:

"Yea, team!
Rah! Rah! Rah!"

Sally was so dumbfounded she could scarcely believe her ears. They were using her silly jingle as a cheer! They must have practiced it at the pep rally which she had avoided. Her jingle! Changed somewhat, but hers nonetheless.

But she had written it only as a joke. She certainly hadn't intended for it to be used to encourage the

Hadley West team against her old school! It made her feel like a traitor, listening to the shouts for Hadley West all around her.

As if in response to those shouts, a Hadley West ball carrier streaked through the Hadley East defensive line to a touchdown. As if this were merely a warm-up, the next time the ball was in Hadley West's possession, the team moved steadily down the field to another touchdown. And another. And another.

When the gun sounded to signal the end of the game, Sally was on her feet with everyone else in the stands. She was shrieking in a kind of delirium of joy. For just a little while nothing else was so important, or so thrilling, as touchdowns for Hadley West. Touchdowns. And victory!

7

Kitchen Date

Reluctant to have all the fun of the afternoon come to an end, Sally asked Jonni to walk home with her.

"I'd like that," Jonni promptly answered.

They were in no hurry to get away from the crowd and the buzzing comments. Sally looked around for Sue, but she was not in sight. To her surprise, she saw Weejee, the young man who worked for Lenore's father. He probably had the day off, Sally decided.

"I wish now I'd gone to the rest of the home games," Sally confided to Jonni. "This was such fun!"

"Except," Jonni pointed out, "it isn't so much fun when the team loses."

Jonni was right. This was their first win. Right now Sue was probably moaning over the disappointment of her school's defeat. Thinking of Sue, Sally felt guilty again as she remembered how thrilled she had been—or had she been shocked—at hearing her words used by the cheerleaders.

She became aware that Judd Clemens was at their heels when he declared, smiling broadly, "Your mother told me to keep an eye on you, Jonni."

She whispered to Sally, "I think it's you he wants to keep an eye on. He's been asking me about you."

Sally was still in a flurry over this when Myron came along, and the four of them stayed together all the way to her house. Then it seemed the right thing to ask the boys to come in for a cold drink.

"After all that yelling," Myron said, "I couldn't turn down an offer of anything liquid, believe me."

That seemed quite amusing, and somehow especially so coming from Myron. The four of them were laughing merrily as Sally led the way into the house by way of the back door. Afterward she chided herself for not taking her guests around to the front, but since the sidewalk leading to the back door was closest, that had seemed the natural way to go in.

Her mother was cleaning vegetables at the sink, but after greeting the guests she excused herself, saying, "You know where the cookies and root beer are, Sally."

As if it was not at all unusual for Sally to bring boys in and feed them! So Sally became calmer, and in just a little while it seemed quite natural to act as hostess and join in the conversation all at one time.

Forgetting that she had meant to keep it secret, she told about her silly jingle.

"The one they used was mine, I know, even though they changed it. The way I wrote it, it went 'We'll be true and do our best.' "

"I like that better," Jonni declared.

"So do I," Judd agreed, smiling admiringly at Sally.

But Myron shook his head. "Not for what they wanted it for. The way Sally wrote it, it's a kind of pledge to the school. On the other hand, 'We know you will do your best' is telling the team we know *they* will do their best."

They argued good-naturedly about this. Sally found the argument stimulating and absorbing, and she was startled at the sound of Lucia's voice from the doorway.

"Jeeks!" Lucia exclaimed. "What's all the noise about?"

For a moment Sally was embarrassed, but soon everyone laughed, and Sally asked, "Would you like some cookies, Lu? Or a drink?"

"I just had water. But I'd like cookies, please. Enough for me and my friend."

Lu had been drinking from the outside faucet again, Sally suspected, so she could pretend to give Horace a drink. But, fortunately, Lu made no reference to Horace. Unless, Sally thought in dismay, the friend she referred to was Horace!

Jonni and Lu exchanged a few comments about how nice it would be to ride a horse on a day like this. Then Lu said very politely to Judd, "It was nice to meet you," and she went running out with a pocketful of cookies.

Judd said, as if he meant it, "Nice kid," and Jonni said, "Yes, isn't she a honey? I wish I had a sister. I have two brothers, both married."

Sally peered somewhat apprehensively out of the window, just in time to see Lu in the act of sharing her cookies with a small girl from the next block. With a relieved sigh she sat back and basked in a feeling of contentment. Maybe she would tell Sue that she'd had a double date today. There were four of them—two girls and two boys. That made it a double date, didn't it? But then she decided that it would be silly to exaggerate her "kitchen date." Besides, Sue was sure to poke fun at mention of Myron in connection with a date.

"Why weren't you in the band today?" she asked Myron.

"They had enough horns, including a sousa. Which was all right with me. I've already had two years of band. Time for something else, maybe."

He was a strange boy, she thought, listening as he and Jonni discussed music. She was rather surprised at how much Jonni seemed to know about music.

Her thoughts wandered back to the game, and now she found it hard to understand why she had been pleased when the new school had defeated the old. For her affection and loyalty were certainly with Hadley East. Yet there was no doubt that after the first half she had wanted Hadley West to win, and she had rejoiced in their victory.

She asked Myron, "Is the real reason you don't want to play in the band because you are still loyal to the old school?"

He looked surprised at her question. "I don't see

that there is any question of loyalty involved between Hadley East and Hadley West."

"But how can you say that?" Sally protested, smarting with the perplexity of her own feelings about school loyalty.

"Well, the way I figure," Myron said, pushing his chair back from the kitchen table the better to stretch his long legs, "the way I figure, it's sort of like the switch from grammar school to junior high, and then from junior high to high. You can still have the old soft spot in the heart for the schools you've left behind."

Before Sally could say it, Judd spoke up. "But there are two high schools involved here. That makes it different. The first high school you go to has just got to seem tops to a guy. I remember how big shot I thought I was when I finally got to high school. It was like—well, sort of like becoming a man. I thought I was grown up for sure, that first day when I walked into Central High."

"In the city?" Sally asked with interest. "You moved here from the city?"

He grinned at her. She liked the way he looked when he grinned: His whole face seemed to join in.

"For the two years that I was at Central, I took it

for granted that it was the world's greatest school and that I'd be there to graduate. Then we got notice that the apartment building we lived in was going to be torn down to make room for another expressway."

Sally was touched at Judd's story, and she was sure he understood how she felt, even if Myron didn't.

Myron insisted, "Yes, but it really isn't the school itself, I mean the buildings and all that, that your loyalty is involved with. It's the people—the teachers as well as the kids. So don't forget, Sally, that the old Hadley isn't the same, because part of it is now included in the new school. So even if you thought you should hate the old school to prove you love the new one, or vice versa, it wouldn't make much sense because the new school is just an offshoot of the old."

"Well, then, smarty," Sally said tartly, "I suppose you think we should all have been cheering for both sides at the game today?"

Myron laughed with the others before answering seriously, "Since you asked me, I think the right way to compete is not *against* something or someone. The best way is to compete with our own past record, to improve it."

Sally was about to say witheringly, just as Sue would have said it, "Well, now I've heard everything!"

But Jonni had jumped to her feet after glancing at the kitchen clock. "Murder; I've got to get home! My mother is working at the store today, and I said I'd have the dinner cooked and ready to go on the table when she steps foot in the door."

She added warmly, "This has been such fun, Sally! I really do wish I didn't have to run. And I love your house. I always did like big old houses."

"You'll have to come back soon," Sally said in her best hostess manner, "and see the rest of it." She wanted Jonni to come back. Poor Jonni, loving big houses and having to live in a crackerbox house!

"How about me?" Judd asked. "Don't I get the tour of inspection?"

"No," Sally answered firmly, "that's for girls only."

For girls only, she mused when the three of them had gone. Judd hadn't taken offense at her quick retort. In fact, he'd seemed to enjoy it. Talking with boys wasn't so very different from talking with girls, although there was *some* difference. And with some boys it would undoubtedly be much more difficult. With Whit, for instance, she admitted, and then tried not to think of Sue's brother for fear it might spoil her feeling of success.

She heard her mother coming, and she busied herself with empty glasses and cookie platters.

"I'll wash these," she said. Noticing the vegetables in the sink, she offered, "And I'll finish cleaning the carrots and beets."

"Well, thank you, Sally. How was your party?" her mother asked.

"Perfect," she decided aloud. "Just perfect. And they liked your cookies. Jonni liked the butterscotch especially, and the boys favored the oatmeal ones."

She did not hear the comment her mother made, for she was busy thinking of just what Jonni and Judd and Myron had said, and especially what had been said about school loyalty.

That reminded her of Lenore, who scoffed at such things as school loyalty. She was glad Lenore hadn't returned home early, as she had threatened her mother she might do. For if Lenore had joined them, things certainly would not have turned out as they did. The boys would have kept their eyes on Lenore, the way boys always did. And Lenore would have made funny remarks, as she always did. She might even have poked fun at Myron.

No, if Lenore had been there, it would not have been such a perfect party.

8

Crackerbox Kid

Sue telephoned to offer her explanation of how it had been possible for the Hadley West team to beat the Hadley East team.

"We were overconfident," Sue said emphatically. "We'd been so keyed up for all those important conference games we've been playing, we were just not in the right mental condition for an unimportant game."

"I know." Sally agreed, even as it occurred to her that it was Sue who had referred to the game between the two Hadley schools as "the big game."

She didn't mention this to Sue. Sue was upset enough over her school's defeat.

"But we'll win our game Saturday with Elmville, of course," Sue predicted. "We'll win the game–and the conference championship."

"That will be wonderful," Sally said. She meant it.

To show that she meant it, she decided to wear her orange and white outfit to school on Friday. It was "Dress-Up Day," and this seemed a doubly good reason for wearing her knit for the first time.

She was prepared for comments. Even boos. If somebody called her a traitor to the new school, she wouldn't let it bother her. Everybody might as well know right now where she stood. She intended to be true to the old school forever, regardless!

The weather had turned colder. In fact there had been a few snowflakes Thursday evening. Sue had phoned once again to confide her worry over the effect a snowfall might have on the game with Elmville. But by school time on Friday, the snowflakes had long since disappeared.

Sally even felt a little too warm, wearing her full-length coat instead of the shorter everyday plaid that just didn't look right with her orange skirt showing below it.

She removed her coat and waited defiantly for comments. Most of the girls near her locker were exchanging compliments. One girl said, "You look darling, too, Sally." Another agreed. "Yes, what a lovely color, Sally! It's so becoming."

They didn't even seem to realize that she was wearing Hadley East colors. Because it was Dress-Up Day, the girls were so busy looking to see what everyone was wearing that school colors didn't even register.

When Lenore saw what had been hidden by Sally's coat she said, "Oh, so that's why you wouldn't let me buy you a sweater."

Lenore might have meant her words as a compliment. Sometimes it was hard to know, with Lenore. Sally felt a little better when Jonni paused long enough to assure her, "You could pose for a fashion magazine! I was almost late because I forgot about Dress-Up and had to run home and change." Jonni thrust out one foot; she was wearing nylons and heels, though her straight skirt and tailored blouse looked familiar. Maybe Jonni just didn't have anything really dress-up to wear, Sally thought pityingly.

It was good to see the boys wearing coats and ties. Even Myron looked better, though of course she couldn't expect him to look at all the way Whit

Fowler looked when he got dressed up. The mere thought of how Whit looked set her to dreaming so that she almost forgot about the telltale colors of her dress.

She was on her way to her last class of the day when Judd Clemens fell into step with her to comment, "I see nobody gave you the bum's rush." He added, at her uncertain look, "For wearing those colors."

She smothered an impulse to laugh, and thought again that Judd was nice. And he was also smart, she decided.

The next day was dreary in more ways than one. Sally wanted to be at Elmville to see Hadley East win the championship. She knew there were no tickets to be had, even if she could find a way of getting there. But she was in no mood for cleaning her room or ironing or the other things she was expected to do on Saturday. Housework was such a bore, she wasn't at all sure that she wanted to get married and do housework the rest of her life.

If she were still at the old school, there would be so many exciting things she could do. As it was, there wasn't even anything to look forward to. Not that there weren't things planned for the students at Hadley West. There was the Harvest Haze dance all the kids were talking about. But nobody had asked her to go. And she probably wouldn't go, even if she were asked.

She wondered if she should write to Bill Stokes, the boy who lived next door to her sister. He had said he would write if she did. But she was not in the mood.

To make the day worse, she and Lucia quarreled. It was Lu's fault, of course. For Lu was carrying on out in the backyard, making like she was clinging to the back of a bucking bronco, whooping and acting like an Indian on the warpath.

Sally felt it her duty to speak plainly to Lu. "If you don't stop acting that way, Lucia Sorenson, the men in the white coats will come and take you away with them."

At first Lu talked back. Then she looked hurt. She even cried a little, and that made Sally feel worse than ever.

By the time she heard the score of the Elmville-Hadley East game, she wanted to duck into a dark corner and do some crying herself. For Elmville—little Elmville—had beaten Hadley East by a score of twenty-seven to thirteen!

The next morning the sun was shining brightly,

but this was no true omen of the day. As if the football catastrophe of the day before hadn't been enough to bear, the telephone rang early with word that the new school building had been defaced with red paint the night before.

Sally was shocked. "Why would anyone want to do a thing like that—daub paint on a nice new building?"

"Destructive acts never make sense—not really," her father said. "Usually these things are done by someone who imagines that this is a way of getting even with someone."

Sally was quick to predict, "I suppose everyone will decide it was kids from the old school who did it because they were sore about the game yesterday and the one last week."

"Or," her father said, "the two groups in the new school who have been at odds might be suspected. There was a fight after the game last week between the so-called Crackerbox Kids and some other boys in your school. But let's not jump to conclusions before we have some substantiating evidence."

He added sternly, "And don't let's say that this was just a harmless prank. Defacing public property is not my idea of a harmless prank."

Sally wanted to talk to Sue about all this. But Sue

was not in church this morning, and when the family returned home she felt hesitant about phoning her friend. Undoubtedly Sue was brokenhearted over Elmville spoiling Hadley East's chance at the championship. And if Sue didn't know about the vandalism, she wasn't sure she wanted to tell her.

While she was hesitating, the telephone rang, and her father returned from answering it looking very serious.

"It seems a boy from your school was seen walking off the grounds with a bucket of paint last night, Sally. It is not likely that one boy could have done it all himself, judging by the extent of the damages. His name is Judd Clemens. Do you know him, Sally?"

"Judd? Of course I know him. He was here last Saturday, with Myron and Jonni—after the game. Judd couldn't have done it! You met him, Mother. He's a nice boy. Isn't he, Mother?"

"He certainly seemed like a nice, polite boy," her mother agreed. "But you know some boys do foolish things at times, Sally."

"Some boys," her father said, "and also some girls."

Sally was in no mood for general observations. It was Judd she wanted to talk about. "They'll probably put the blame on Judd because he's one of the Crackerbox Kids," she muttered disgustedly.

Her father answered seriously, "The evidence against him has nothing to do with where he lives, Sally. The incriminating evidence is the fact that he was on the scene with a bucket of red paint. That is what makes things look bad for him."

As soon as dinner was over Sally headed for the upstairs extension phone. She must phone Sue, if only to be certain that Sue did not accept as true any rumors about Judd Clemens.

"There must be some mistake," she told Sue. "I'm sure Judd just couldn't do a thing like that."

Sue had her doubts. "How can you tell what the Crackerbox Kids might do? I'm glad they caught him. If they hadn't, everybody was sure to blame our school."

Sue sounded so sure that nobody from *her* school could be involved in defacing the new school. Sally felt resentment rising, and she almost said, "The kids at our school are just as good as the kids at your school! Just as good as the kids from Robinswood, too!"

When they ended the conversation she was glad she'd held her tongue. Not that she didn't know that the Crackerbox Kids were as good as anyone. They were, of that she was sure. Jonni, and Judd, and all the rest of them. But it was so confusing to talk of two schools. My school. Our school. Your school. Which was which?

She became aware that her sister had been lingering near the top of the staircase.

Lu spoke diffidently. "Sally?"

"What?" Sally repeated the word, aware that Lu looked troubled, and she didn't want to be quarreling with her little sister all the time. "What, Lu?"

Words tumbled from Lucia's lips. "I saw something last night. I wanted to tell someone right away, but I didn't know if I should."

Sally made an extra effort to be patient. "So you saw something. What did you see?"

Lucia tugged at a pigtail, usually a sign of concentration. "It was after supper. I knew I shouldn't have gone. But I went back to look for Horace's whip. I'd lost it—"

"Horace's whip!" Sally almost shouted the words. At a time like this, when she was so upset, her little sister had to start chattering about Horace! "Aren't you ever going to stop that silly make-believe?"

She was sorry when she saw the hurt look on Lu's face. Hurrying to the privacy of her own room, she told herself she had said what she had said for Lu's own good.

After all, nobody should expect to stay in a dream world forever!

9

Sunday Visit

"I'm going for a walk," Sally stopped at the door of the den to inform her parents.

Lucia had gone out. On her walk she might see her and make up with her. She couldn't stand to stay in the house one more minute. She certainly couldn't put her mind on schoolwork. Yesterday she had been awaiting the outcome of the football game. Today there was all this other excitement to keep her from concentrating on math and Spanish and world history.

A walk might clear away some of the confusing

questions that were plaguing her. Questions about Judd and the bucket of paint. Questions about Sue and *her* school. Questions about Lucia and that silliness with Horace. Why couldn't everything be all plain and sensible, instead of getting so all mixed up?

Without realizing that she was headed in that direction, she found herself nearing the crackerbox section; and she kept going, determined to see what it was like. She would go to see Jonni. She had asked her many times. Jonni had reminded her, "We live at one-two-three Wonder Road. One-two-three. That's easy to remember. Wonder how it could be any easier. There you have it—one-two-three Wonder Road."

Sally found Wonder Road without any difficulty. She saw that though the houses in this new section were modest, they were all well-cared-for. She could see no reason why anyone should object to these homes or the people in them. What difference did it make that the buildings had been "shells," with some inside work to be completed by the buyers?

Anyone who objected to someone because of buying a house like these was just an old snob, Sally decided, noting approvingly the new plantings of trees and shrubs and evergreens all along the way.

By the time she reached Jonni's house she realized that she was no longer in the crackerbox section, but in an area shaded by fine old trees. The Edwards home, and those neighboring it, were small but with a definite look of quality.

Jonni was at hand to welcome her before the door chimes had ceased echoing through the house.

"Sally, how nice!" Jonni cried. "Mother and I were wishing we'd get some company this afternoon."

Mrs. Edwards had evidently been playing the fine old grand piano beside the windows at the far end of the living room. She came to shake hands with Sally.

"Jonell speaks of you often," Mrs. Edwards said with a warm smile. She had the look of a person who smiled easily, yet there were lines on her face that seemed to indicate that she had known great weariness and sadness.

"I decided to take a walk," Sally said.

Mrs. Edwards's smile deepened. "Mr. Edwards decided to take a Sunday walk also."

After a while she mentioned that Jonni's father had been seriously ill before they moved to Linden. She added quickly, "He is doing just fine now. So well, in fact, that we decided he should be getting back into business again. That is why we started a little book shop in town."

Sally said, "I noticed you have lots of books."

There were shelves full. And there were fine paintings on the walls. It was a beautiful room, she decided, though none of the furnishings were new or in the modern style. Everything was quite unlike Lenore's house. But it was beautiful just the same.

Mrs. Edwards excused herself and went to another part of the house. The two girls sat on a small sofa near the fireplace. Instead of the usual skirt and blouse, today Jonni was wearing a dress made of a dark red silk that was very becoming.

Sally could scarcely wait to ask, "You've heard what happened to Judd Clemens?"

Jonni nodded. "His sister phoned to tell me."

Sally had not even known he had a sister. "He couldn't have done it," she declared emphatically.

"Of course not," Jonni agreed calmly. "He'd been setting pins at the old bowling alley on County Line Road, and he was passing the school on his way home when a convertible full of boys drove away. Unfortunately for him, it didn't occur to him that he might need to identify the boys or the car. He tripped over a paint can, picked it up to dispose of it, and he had it in his hands when someone saw him with it and jumped to the conclusion that he was guilty."

They discussed all the possibilities. Sally admired Jonni's cool logic, and she soon felt calmer, more confident that everyone would eventually realize Judd's innocence.

They talked of other things. Sally asked about the oil painting over the fireplace. "The girl looks like you," she observed, and felt a little awed when Jonni said she had posed for the picture.

"The artist is a friend of my father's. It was done about two years ago. I imagine I've changed a little since then."

Jonni went on to mention a book she'd enjoyed, and she offered to let Sally borrow it.

"If you see anything else you'd like, help yourself," Jonni said with a sweep of her arm toward the shelves of books. She added with a smile, "Father says he bought a book store in self-defense."

Mrs. Edwards returned to the room to turn on a lamp. "It is getting dark much too early to suit me. It would be so nice if you'd stay and have Sunday supper with us, Sally. We haven't been having much company, and we'd all enjoy having you."

With a guilty glance at her watch, Sally pulled

herself from the deep cushions of the small sofa. "I wish I could," she sighed, "but I haven't finished my homework, so I just can't."

Mrs. Edwards's smile was understanding. "Then perhaps, if it is all right with your mother, you might come home with Jonell after school tomorrow and have mustgos with us?"

"Mustgos?" she repeated uncertainly. She was not sure if she should commit herself to eating some hot foreign food which she might not like.

Jonni explained that "mustgos" was her mother's term for things in the refrigerator that "must go," and tomorrow night it would be cold fried chicken that must go.

As she headed homeward, a smile tugged at Sally's lips. The day was not only getting darker, but colder. She buttoned her coat up close to her neck, but it was an automatic act, for she did not feel the cold. She was warm with the remembrance of her visit with Jonni. Jonni was different from anyone she had ever known. In a way she seemed older. Yet in other ways she almost seemed younger. When she talked with Lu about horses, for example, she and Lu seemed much the same age. Nevertheless, Jonni had had her portrait painted by a real live artist. Probably not even Ann Ainsley, Sue's friend from Robinswood, had had that experience! Just wait until she told Sue about all this! Sue had called Jonni "the horse girl." Well, just wait until she told Sue! About the portrait. And the grand piano with sheet music stacked high on it. And all the books, including the one Jonni had let her borrow. She would have plenty to tell Sue, when next they talked. Most important of all, she could now tell Sue that Judd really was innocent, and when they found out who was in the convertible Judd had seen, then they would know who really was guilty.

She would wait until after dinner tomorrow night to tell Sue. She was sure her parents would not object to her having "mustgos" with Jonni. They would be pleased when they heard about her visit today, she was sure.

She was humming contentedly as she neared home. The humming halted abruptly, to become a stifled scream, as Lucia's bicycle almost ran into her.

"Lu! What are you trying to do?"

"Oh, I'm sorry," Lu apologized, looking and sounding truly sorry. "I've been riding around and around, trying to find you, Sally. Since it started to get dark I've been walking with my bike."

For a panicky moment Sally thought something

might have happened to one or both of her parents.

"What is it, Lu? What's happened?"

Lucia heaved a great sigh. "I've just got to tell somebody, Sally." In a quavering voice she added, "There isn't anyone else I can tell. Not about this."

10

Unwelcome Knowledge

Calm again, Sally was sure that nothing Lu might say could possibly disturb her.

"Shoot then. I'm listening."

She was even rather pleased that Lu had brought her problem, whatever it was, to her. She really didn't want Lucia to shut her out of her little world, whacky though that world might be at times.

They started walking slowly, each one grasping a handlebar of Lucia's bicycle to direct it homeward.

"Well—" Lucia gulped. "I went to the high school

last night." She stopped uncertainly.

Sally was puzzled. "There wasn't anything going on at school last night."

"I know. But I went there—"

Sally interrupted. "On your bike, you mean? At night? Oh, Lu!"

The rules as to when and where Lucia was allowed to ride her bike were strictly enforced. Sally said regretfully, "I'm sorry, Lu, but if you broke the rules you'll just have to confess and—"

"Oh, it's not that!" Lucia hastened to assure her. "I didn't ride. I walked."

She explained. "When I went to put my bike away after supper, I couldn't find Horace's—I couldn't find the whip. The one from out West. I was sure I'd had it on the handlebar. But it wasn't there."

"You mean you went out after dark to look for the whip?" Despite her good intentions, a note of exasperation crept into Sally's words.

Lu was defensive. "I was riding at the school in the afternoon. I ride there a lot, on the sidewalk that goes all around the school. You know that, Sally. But not after dark. I know better than that, I hope. I didn't even want to walk in the dark. But I couldn't just let Horace's whip be lost, could I? After we brought it all the way from out West and everything?"

Lu was almost in tears, and Sally hastened to say consolingly, "No, I guess you couldn't, Lu." After all, this was her little sister. She didn't want to be an old meanie to her little sister.

Lu sniffed hard before going on. "I walked all around the school because I'd ridden all around on my bike, the way I always do when I go there to ride. Then I heard this car, and I didn't want anyone else scolding me, so I ducked behind the school sign."

With a twinge of conscience, Sally suspected that she was the one who, according to Lu, had been "scolding."

Lu's voice rose as she said, "When I heard things crash against the school building, I was scared."

"You heard things crash?" Sally asked uncertainly. Was Lu trying to tell her that she had been a witness to the vandalism the night before? "You mean you saw who did it?"

"Well, no, not really." Lu tugged at a pigtail. "But I heard them, Sally. I heard the crashing. And I heard voices. Boys' voices."

"How many?" Sally demanded, thinking of Judd. It was almost too good to be true! She might be the one to free Judd!

"Four. Or maybe five. I'm not sure."

It hadn't been Judd, Sally thought exultantly. She'd been sure all along, of course. Now everyone would know it had not been Judd Clemens. They'd be sorry, all those who had been so ready to condemn a Crackerbox Kid. Or they'd better be sorry.

Lu went on. "And I heard the funny sound the car made. Like something was sure to shake loose any minute."

A boy had been driving an old heap, Sally decided.

"And," Lu continued, "I heard one boy yell, 'Crank her up! Blast off!' "

Sally's steps halted abruptly. "You heard—what?"

Lu repeated the words. "Crank her up! Blast off!"

More than once Sally had heard Whit Fowler use those very words. But Whit couldn't be involved in a thing like this!

But Corny Cobb's convertible often sounded as if a fender or something was about to fall off.

She could believe that Corny might be mixed up in what had occurred the night before. But not Whit! Not Sue's brother! Not Whit! There must be some horrible mistake somewhere.

Lu stopped tugging her pigtail and reached out to touch Sally's hand.

"What are we going to do, Sally?" she asked worriedly.

"I don't know," she admitted. "I don't know."

Suddenly she shivered. The blackness of night was drawing close. Cold winds were blowing all around. She wanted to get home. Right away.

11

Good Sport

For once, Lenore was right on time, waiting to walk to school. Sally wished she could stay at home. She was still upset over what Lucia had told her the day before. And she still didn't know what she should do. She wished she could leave town and get away from it all. She wished she could go back to Oregon and visit her sister Linda. Maybe Linda could tell her what she should do.

Lenore had been to a wedding over the weekend, and she started at once to tell Sally all about the bride's dress, the bridesmaids' dresses, and the flower girls' dresses.

All this was of no interest to Sally at the moment, and she was moved to speak of that which she had not intended to mention.

"Did you hear that somebody splashed paint all over the school Saturday evening?"

Lenore's eyebrows rose slightly. She laughed a little. "That right?"

Sally confided that Judd was under suspicion. "But he didn't do it. Judd just wouldn't do a crazy thing like that. It's just circumstantial evidence against him."

The rest of what she knew, what Lucia had told her—this she did not even want to think about. She felt all sick inside whenever she thought about it. The evidence against Whit—wasn't it circumstantial, too? She wanted to hear somebody agree with her. Without meaning to, she found herself speaking of things she had not meant to speak about. The words seemed to come from her mouth of their own accord, against her wishes.

"What would you do, Lenore, if you had been told—something—something that would be damaging evidence against someone you know—"

She could say no more, and she wondered if she should have spoken at all. She didn't want anyone questioning her as to what she knew. She didn't want to do or say anything that might hurt Whit.

Lenore asked indifferently, "You mean something about the school getting messed up with paint?"

Sally nodded.

Lenore said lightly, "Forget it, I'd say. It's not your problem. Why sweat over it?"

"Well—it's just that it's not fair for Judd to get the blame when he's innocent."

"Innocent—guilty—who cares?" Lenore scoffed. "Kids do stuff like that all the time. So why sweat over it?"

Just then Myron came trotting along to join them with a cheerful "Morning, gals."

Sally answered with an automatic "Hi." Her thoughts were on Lenore. Didn't the girl have any sense of justice? Didn't she understand how Judd must feel, being accused of something he hadn't done? No wonder Lenore's brothers were such little monsters, disliked by everyone in the neighborhood. Apparently Mr. and Mrs. Andres hadn't taught their children right from wrong.

Lenore referred again to the wedding she had

attended. "The shade of blue the bride wore was dreamy for her, but I'd rather have ice blue. And ice green for the bridesmaids. That would be cool plus. Can't you see it, Sally?"

"Cool as ice," Sally answered without enthusiasm, while she wondered that a fifteen-year-old girl—even one going on sixteen—should be so interested in weddings. This was not the first time Lenore had carried on about what she would wear at her wedding.

Myron asked, "Now that you've decided about the dress, Lenore, how about the fellow? Have you decided on him, too?"

Lenore shot an angry glance his way. "Maybe I have, smarty. Old smarty long legs!"

Myron continued to smile, but Sally was sure his ears reddened. She hastened to say, "Being tall has lots of advantages."

"Name one," Lenore snapped. "Besides replacing the ladder."

Sally wanted to laugh at that. Lenore could be so funny sometimes! But she didn't dare laugh at Myron.

"Well—" She thought of obvious answers. "Being able to see in a crowd, for one. Or playing basketball. Are you going out for the team, Myron?"

"Could be," he said with a grin that made her

doubt that he was being serious. Then she remembered that he had played on the junior high team. But this only made her more uncertain that he could be speaking seriously for he had not played on the freshman team at Hadley East.

He was serious, though, as he spoke of what had been done to the school building on Saturday. If Lenore was indifferent about this, Myron certainly was not.

"Whoever did it, I sure don't think they should be allowed to get away with it. Anyone big enough to do what they did is old enough to know better. A school building is public property and—"

Lenore interrupted. "So it belongs to all of us!"

"To use for the purpose it was intended for," Myron resumed promptly. "But not for any one of us to wreck it. If we all own it, then we should all protect our common interest in it, I'd say."

"You sound like some old preacher," Lenore scoffed. "I bet you were a little goodie-goodie when you were a kid."

She hurried ahead of them and into the school building, not lingering with the crowd gathered at the main entrance to examine the daubs and streaks and splatters of bright red that defaced the new structure. Everyone was talking excitedly.

Sally stared at the damage. The nice new building now looked pretty awful—as awful as her Easter suit had looked when she spilled nail polish on it. And she felt just as unhappy, gazing at the front of the school, as she had felt when she examined her suit all streaked with pink polish.

She had forgotten Myron, and at first his voice beside her was just one more voice in the crowd, all of them upset, some of them angry, many of them muttering threats against those responsible for the outrage. There were many muttered references to Hadley East. It was generally agreed that someone from the old school was responsible for marring the appearance of the new school.

Myron spoke quietly, for Sally's ears only.

"Do you suppose she thinks her young brothers might have done it—or had a hand in it?"

For a moment Sally made no sense from his words.

Then she gasped. "The little monsters? But they're just—"

Just kids, she had been about to say. But, possibly, big enough to have done this. Especially if one or two others had helped. But what others? Royal and Junior were not very popular—even with boys of their own age or older. On the other hand, they were the kind who might have done it. And if the monsters were guilty, that meant Whit Fowler was not involved after all!

For just a little while she felt relieved, almost happy. All too soon she had to return to what Lucia had told her. Lu had heard a car. She had heard voices. Little monsters or not, it seemed most unlikely that Royal and Junior were among the boys in the rattly old car.

With a sigh, she went to her locker. Jonni was waiting there for her.

"You haven't forgotten about tonight?" Jonni asked with a smile.

She had forgotten. She had completely forgotten to ask her mother if she might go home with Jonni for "mustgos."

"Oh, Jonni, I'm sorry!" she apologized. "I've been so mixed up on account of that horrid red paint!" She asked anxiously, "What about Judd? Have they cleared him?"

"Not that I've heard. I'm sorry you're not coming. Do you suppose you could phone your mother and get permission?"

"I'll see," Sally agreed, but without enthusiasm.

With her thoughts so full of what might happen to Whit, she had no desire to go to Jonni's.

At midmorning a special assembly was called. All the boys and girls, usually full of chatter, seemed subdued as they filed into the auditorium. Sally tried not to listen to the whispered comments of the girls on either side of her. These girls had heard rumors. Somebody was about to get it, but good! Why else had a special assembly been called?

Sally shivered. Who was going to "get it"? Judd? Whit?

She kept her eyes on the platform, waiting for Mr. Hardie to appear. He had been assistant principal at the old school. He and her parents were on friendly terms. One day, near the beginning of the first month of school, Mr. Hardie had stopped her in the hall to ask if her father had caught any fish on their vacation. Lenore, who had been with her, had been wide-eyed, as if being on friendly terms with a school principal was something very much outside her experience.

The auditorium was unnaturally still as Mr. Hardie started to speak. He was not a very big man, but he had a firm voice and a good delivery.

"I feel that I should say a few things to you about sportsmanship," he said in his brisk, firm way. "And about loyalty. Or perhaps I should say about misdirected loyalty. For there have been indications of this among us here."

Sally felt as if she were suddenly freezing solid, so that she could scarcely hear or breathe. Was Mr. Hardie about to accuse Judd? "Some of us here," he had said. That couldn't mean Whit or Corny. That must mean Judd. Or, more likely, the boys her father had mentioned? The boys who had been disciplined for brawling after the Hadley East-Hadley West game?

As Mr. Hardie continued speaking she waited for him to mention names. She found it difficult to concentrate on what he was saying, but she gathered that he was stressing that the best way to show loyalty to a school was to be a credit to the school.

That sounded familiar. Something like what Myron had said. Had he got it from Mr. Hardie?

She really listened now as Mr. Hardie said, "Some of you wanted to stay at the old school. That is understandable. You had a sense of loyalty to the old school. But things change in this life. Some of these changes can't be helped. But you, as individuals, can help your attitude toward these changes. You can make the changes an opportunity for self-improvement. You can contribute your efforts to see that the changes work for the best interests of all concerned. That is being a good sport."

A good sport, Sally thought wonderingly. Have I been a good sport?

Her attention returned to Mr. Hardie, who was saying, "If you try to take out your disappointment by picking on others, by quarrels, by senseless destructive acts such as spoiling the appearance of school property—that is poor sportsmanship. I hope each one of you will examine your thinking and your actions, so there will be no further instances such as the one which took place here on Saturday evening. . . ."

Again Sally was sure Mr. Hardie was going to mention names. When the assembly was dismissed, she could scarcely believe that no names had been mentioned.

Everyone seemed to know about Judd, judging by the remarks around her as she and the others made their way up the aisles. Everyone seemed sure of Judd's innocence. But was Mr. Hardie sure of Judd's innocence?

That was the question that haunted Sally all day. Whenever she thought of Mr. Hardie's definition of a good sport, she had an uneasy feeling that she could not qualify. But mostly she wondered how Judd was to prove his innocence. Especially if she did not tell what she knew.

Several times Judd seemed to be heading her way, and because she could not bear to face him, she managed to avoid him. Before her last class he was standing near the classroom door. This time she had to face him.

Cautiously she said, "Hi," and hoped he would let her pass.

He made it plain that he had no intention of letting her pass. He said, "I just wanted to be sure you were still speaking to me."

It had not occurred to her to think how her avoidance of him might look to him—as if she had decided he was guilty!

"Of course I'm speaking to you," she declared firmly. "And I don't believe you are guilty, if that's what you mean."

The changed look on Judd's face, and his slightly crooked but wonderful smile, warmed her spirits. She marched into the classroom. Her head was now held high.

But if Judd wasn't guilty, someone else was.

Much as she didn't want to, she was going to have to talk to Sue. She was going to have to tell Sue what

Lucia had seen and heard. She could think of no other way.

It wasn't going to be easy to tell Sue. But she had to do it. She had to be a good sport.

12

Broken Friendship

To avoid having to walk home with anyone, Sally hurried to her locker when the bell rang. She didn't want to talk about the assembly. Snatching her coat and the books she would be needing, she made her way out a side door. A fleeting glimpse of Jonni almost halted her steps. She had forgotten about telephoning her mother. She also had forgotten Jonni would be waiting to know if she were going home with her.

At the moment she felt that she mustn't stop for

anyone or anything. Not even to apologize to Jonni. For if she stopped, she might lose her courage to say what she knew she must say to Sue. So she dared not speak to Jonni or anyone else, except for an answering "Hi" to those who spoke as she passed them on her way to the corner where Sue should get off the bus.

If Sue wasn't on the bus, Sally was not sure what she would do next. She just couldn't go to Sue's, for fear of running into Whit. Facing Sue was going to be hard enough. For her to face Whit would be more than she could bear.

The corner where the bus stopped was a pleasant spot. In every direction there were smooth lawns, with grass not yet browned by a killing frost. Masses of asters and chrysanthemums waved colorful heads in the rather chilly breeze. Sally had eyes only for the stretch of macadam along which the big yellow school bus would arrive. When at last it came to a smooth stop close to the curb, Sally almost hoped Sue was not on the bus so she could hurry home.

Sue spotted her at once. She looked pleased to see her. She also looked very pretty, in a new brown outfit with a jaunty short coat.

"Sally! I was just thinking about you! I hope you can come home with me."

Sue, her best friend, had been thinking about her! This fact made it even harder to say, "No, I can't, Sue. There is something—something I must tell you right now."

"Sally, is something wrong? You don't look right."

Sue looked so concerned, it made Sally want to cry.

"Let's get out of the way," she suggested, motioning to a hedge-bordered driveway where they could step out of earshot of people passing by.

Looking puzzled, Sue went with her.

"Now," she said, "what is it? Don't keep me in suspense, Sally."

She forced out the words she had been rehearsing.

"It's about the paint that was smeared on our school. I found out something about it—about who did it—and I just don't know what to do about it, Sue!"

"Oh, poor Sally," Sue sympathized. "How horrible for you! We got a lecture in assembly today about the paint. As if we were all responsible. As if our school had done it. By the time assembly was dismissed we were all beginning to feel as if we actually had done it. It was a regular brainwash, believe me, Sally."

It was plain that Sue was confident that Hadley

East students had had no part in the vandalism. And, listening to her, Sally wondered if perhaps her sister might have been mistaken somehow. For Lucia had been mistaken about Horace's whip; this morning she had found it, safe in the back yard.

Sally blurted out unhappily, "Lu heard the boys who did it. She heard them talking. She heard a car."

Sue shifted her schoolbooks from her left arm to her right. She spoke uncertainly. "Lucia saw—"

"No." Sally corrected her. "She didn't see them because she hid behind the school sign. You know, the one near the front entrance. She hid there when she heard the boys and their car."

Sue's slight frown deepened. "You mean she recognized their voices?"

"No."

"Then the car— She recognized the car?"

"She didn't see it. But she said it sounded as if a fender or something was about to fall off it."

Sue gasped, and quickly pretended she hadn't. "Well, I don't think that's much if she didn't see the car. Lots of boys have old heaps that make quite a racket sometimes."

Sue had thought of Corny's car at once, Sally knew. She couldn't blame Sue for not wanting to admit it.

Reluctantly, Sally persisted. "Lu also heard a boy say, 'Crank her up! Blast off!' "

In a quick, jerky motion, Sue thrust her armload of books toward Sally, as if to push her away. Her voice shook. "You're just making that up!"

"No," Sally said sadly. "It's true."

Sue was angry now. "True? Who says it's true? Just because that awful sister of yours—"

"Lucia is not awful," Sally said frostily.

"All right, maybe she isn't. But she certainly can't be trusted. You know that, Sally."

"I know no such thing, Sue Fowler. Lucia is honest—"

"Well, all right then, she's honest. Maybe she doesn't cheat, if that's what you mean. But she makes up things all the time. You can't deny that, Sally Sorenson!"

"Yes, but she wouldn't make up something like this! It's just when she's playing—"

"And what was she doing at your school after dark? I'll bet she was playing, wasn't she?"

"No, she was looking for Horace's—" Sally corrected herself quickly. "She was looking for something she'd lost."

"A likely story!" Sue snorted. "If you think I'm

going to tell a story like that to—to anyone, you're very much mistaken, Sally Sorenson. I think you're just trying to protect that crackerbox boy. I think you've got a crush on him, and you're trying to save him, that's what I think."

Sally was suddenly so furious that she wanted to reach out and grab a handful of Sue's hair. "You'd better tell Whit. That is why I waited to talk to you—so you'll tell Whit."

Anger distorted Sue's pretty face. "Why should I tell him? Why should I tell Whit the silly things your silly sister imagined? Besides, Whit wouldn't do a thing like that! He wouldn't be mixed up in anything like that! Especially now, when Daddy is talking about letting him have a car of his own again."

This all but overwhelmed Sally. If it was true that Whit was involved in this horrible thing, it might deprive him of the car he'd been wanting so desperately.

"I'm sorry," Sally gasped. "But please, please tell Whit."

If he wasn't guilty, he could probably prove his innocence. That was no more than right.

Sue did not agree. "You just don't want to believe that Whit is innocent. But you stick up for that crackerbox boy! And I thought you were a friend of mine!"

Sue thrust her books toward Sally again, as if to strike her. For just a moment Sally almost wished Sue would hit her so she could hit back.

Then Sue turned away, declaring brokenly, "I never want to see you again, Sally Sorenson!"

Choking with tears, Sally ran home.

13

Operation Rag Time

She had done all she was going to do about the situation, Sally told herself that night and again the next day. She had tried to talk Sue into telling Whit. What more could anyone ask of her?

All too plainly she saw that Lucia expected her to do something more, though what, Lu did not say. Lu just looked at her. A look that reproached her, and annoyed her, and made her feel altogether miserable.

She was sure her parents suspected that something was amiss.

"You girls are unnaturally quiet," her father remarked at the dinner table.

"You aren't eating very much," her mother commented.

But they asked no questions, though Lucia's tight-lipped reaction was enough to set anyone to questioning, Sally was sure.

When everyone had finished eating, Sally said, "I'll do the dishes tonight."

If she'd known her generosity was going to cause so much commotion she would have held her tongue.

Her mother said, "It's not your turn, Sally."

"I know," she said.

Her father said, "The millennium must have arrived! One of you girls offering to do a chore out of turn!"

Most upsetting of all was Lucia's indignation.

"That's right, it's not your turn, Sally. You're being unfair!" Lucia accused.

That was too much. "Unfair?" she yelped. "I was trying to be nice. And that's the thanks I get!"

She stalked off to her room and her homework. It was almost time for the first quarter exams, and she wanted her grades to be as good or better than they'd been last year, though everything seemed to be conspiring to keep her thoughts in a turmoil.

When the phone rang, she almost toppled her desk chair in her eagerness to answer it. Her heart pounded with the hope that Sue might be calling. Or someone who would say that everything had been resolved and the guilty ones had turned out to be somebody she didn't even know.

Her father had answered the downstairs phone and he was calling her name.

"For you, Sally."

She lifted the receiver with a breathless "Hello?"

"Hi, Sally. This is Judd," a nice boyish voice said.

"Oh! Judd!" What did he want? Had he somehow found out that Lucia had some information? Would he want her to admit what she knew? But she didn't know anything, really. And she certainly didn't want to be a tattletale!

"I just wanted to say thanks," Judd said.

"Thanks—for what?"

"Because you believe me. Because you don't think I had anything to do with that mess Saturday night."

"Why, no, of course I don't," she answered weakly, and could think of nothing further to say.

There was an awkward silence on the line.

At last Judd said, "Sally?"

"Yes?"

"Would you— Well, would you— Do you think it would be asking too much of a girl—" Words came in a sudden rush: "Do you think it would be wrong for me to expect a girl to have enough faith in me to —well, say like go to the Harvest Haze dance with me?"

Astonishment tied her tongue completely. All she could manage was a strangled sound that even she was not able to interpret.

Judd hastened to say, "Of course I probably should wait for the mess to be straightened out. I suppose I really shouldn't ask. . . ."

His voice trailed off. She wanted to offer reassurance. Of course she would like to go to the Harvest Haze dance that marked the end of the football season. And of course she would go with Judd, if he wanted to take her. But she was not certain if he had actually asked to take her to the dance, or if he merely wanted to ask if she thought it would be right for him to ask *a* girl. Some other girl? Jonni, perhaps?

She stammered, "I don't know why any girl wouldn't be glad to go with you, Judd."

He said, "Well, thanks, Sally." He didn't sound altogether pleased with her answer.

In a little while he said, "See you in school tomorrow."

She put the phone down slowly. A boy had telephoned her for a date—or had he? Ordinarily she would have been thrilled at having a boy phone—especially a boy as nice as Judd. In her present state, everything seemed to come out all mixed up.

If only things could somehow return to the way they had been when they left for their vacation. But that would mean she wouldn't know Jonni. Or Judd. Or Lenore. On the other hand, it would mean she and Sue would still be friends.

She sighed, a sigh that had to be hauled painfully all the way from the tips of her flat-heeled shoes.

At bedtime she couldn't sleep. She heard her mother come upstairs, but not her father, and after a while she got out of bed and peered down the dark hall. A finger of light in the downstairs hall told her that her father was still in his den, so she stole quietly down the stairs.

He looked up from the papers on his desk with a start. "Sally? I thought you were in bed."

"I was. But I guess I'll never sleep unless I tell something."

He pulled an upholstered chair close and said, "Sit

here; you'll be warmer. Sure you're not cold?"

"Not really. I mean—just nervous cold." Even a fur coat over her pajamas wouldn't shut out the cold of being nervous about what she had to say.

When she did not speak he said, "I hope you have some information as to where those parlay cards have been coming from. They showed up again at last Saturday's game. A high school game is no place for betting."

As he spoke he adjusted the desk lamp so that it was directed away from her face. She was glad he was so understanding at times. His remarks about the betting cards were intended to put her at ease, she suspected.

"Might as well get it off your chest, Sally," he advised. "Whatever it is that is bothering you."

"I haven't heard anything about betting but—well, I do want to tell you something else," she answered. "But I can't tell you the names. I just can't. But I realize somebody has to do something about it. I mean, about the paint at school."

He was quiet for a moment before saying, "Whatever you know, I certainly agree that you should tell it, with or without names."

So she told about the paint cans crashing, but she didn't say who had hurled them or who had heard them crash. She told about the car that made a rattling noise, but she didn't mention Corny. She told that the words "Crank her up! Blast off!" had been overheard, but she was careful not to say that Whit Fowler had been known to use these very words.

Relieved at having told what she knew, she hurried back to bed. She had done all she felt that she could do. She didn't want to talk about it any more. Her father had an uncanny way of putting facts together. He would come up with the right answers and pass those answers on to the right people. Then perhaps the guilty ones would confess, whoever they were.

The first she knew that the case was resolved was when the *Linden Leader* was delivered several days later. There, on the front page of the paper, under a big headline, was the story. Boys suspected of being involved with the school vandalism had been questioned, and had confessed. They had agreed to make financial restitution for the damages. But, equally as important in the eyes of the newspaper, the boys had offered to remove the marks of their escapade themselves.

No names were mentioned "because of the ages of the youths involved," the paper stated. "Also, we would like to feel that they have learned their lesson. Learned it the hard way, perhaps. Which often is a very lasting way to learn such things, we have found."

In a box in an adjoining column there was an invitation for pupils of both schools, Hadley East and Hadley West, who felt so disposed, and as an indication of a better feeling between the schools than that indicated by the splashed paint, to join in the project with cleaning rags and paint thinner. "Operation Rag Time," the newspaper called it.

Now, more than ever, Sally felt sure that she had done the right thing. But, more than ever, she was sure that her friendship with Sue had ended.

As for Whit, she dared not even think about him. Nor did she ask her father the names of the boys involved. She didn't want to know. If it was true that Whit was one of the guilty ones, she would rather not know about it.

And though she heartily approved of Operation Rag Time, and she hoped that lots of kids from both schools would pitch in and help, she decided that it would be better for her to stay away.

14

Shopping Spree

Thanksgiving Day meant not only turkey and dressing and cranberry sauce and candied sweet potatoes and pumpkin pie, but also a special church service with emphasis on the importance of being grateful.

Sally tried to count her blessings, but her thoughts kept turning to Sue. She had neither seen nor talked with Sue since their quarrel, and she missed her terribly. If she and Sue were still friendly, it wouldn't matter so much that she had muffed a chance to go to the Harvest Haze dance. She and Sue could have laughed about the whole silly affair, including Myron's invitation.

Myron and Judd had walked up to her at school, and Myron had said, "I don't suppose you'd care to go to the dance, Sally?"

If Myron had been alone, she might have said, "Of course I'd like to go." Then he could have taken it from there.

But Judd was with him. And she still hadn't figured out whether Judd had meant to invite her, the night he'd phoned. Now she didn't know if Myron was asking her to go with him, or just asking if she'd care to go, period.

The best answer she could think of was, "Not this time." She waited for Judd to say, "I already asked Sally." Then she could have pretended she'd known it all along. And then she'd have gone with Judd.

As it turned out, she didn't go at all. Jonni went. Lenore didn't go, but that was very little comfort to Sally, for Lenore could certainly have gone with any number of boys if she wanted to go, Sally was sure.

According to Jonni, the dance was a big success. It was sponsored by a girls' club similar to one at Hadley East. Jonni had joined the club, and Sally might have joined if Lenore had not poked so much fun at the idea. "It's just another old maids' society," Lenore scoffed.

Her mother was puzzled as to why she hadn't joined.

"It's a normal part of high school days," Mrs. Sorenson insisted. "Belonging to clubs of the right sort can help a girl learn to get along with others."

"I get along all right without joining any old club," Sally declared defensively, and then she thought of Sue. So many things made her think of Sue. They weren't getting along, of course. And she sometimes didn't get along well with her sister Lu. Maybe she really needed the club. But it was probably too late now to join.

When her father said he wanted to talk to her in private, she wondered uneasily if he was about to say something to add to her unhappiness.

Instead he said, "Your mother and I have decided it is time for you to have a clothing allowance, Sally."

This she could scarcely believe. She was to be allowed to use her mother's charge-a-plate! And, as if this were not enough, she could now pick out her clothes by herself, if she preferred, as of course she did.

"We learn," her father said, "by doing."

She was ecstatic. "Oh, Daddy, that's wonderful! I

need a new coat, you know. That will be number one on my list. And dress shoes. And a couple of skirts." There were many, many other items she needed, of course.

"One thing you must remember," her father warned. "And that is to add up your purchases each time, so you don't go over your quarterly clothes allowance. If you go over, we may have to go back to the old system."

She couldn't allow that to happen. She would feel as if she'd been put back into kindergarten. "I'll be ever so careful," she assured him.

She couldn't wait to tell Lenore. They arranged to go shopping the very next day. She found that now she didn't mind saying, "You can do your shopping at the Flair Shop if you want to, Lenore, but I can't afford it on my allowance."

Lenore seemed to find that amusing. "I'll go wherever you go. I need some slips and stuff."

Weejee was again their chauffeur, and when the two girls stepped out of the car Sally turned back to say, "Thank you, Weejee."

His head snapped her way. Even on this wintry day he wore dark glasses. For the first time he smiled at her. "Sure, kid," he said.

To Lenore he remarked, "Maybe you could learn some manners from your friend, huh?"

Lenore sniffed, a loud sniff. "And maybe you should keep your big mouth shut," she told him.

Sally felt embarrassed, but Weejee's laughter followed them to the door of the store, and Lenore looked pleased.

"One of these days," Lenore declared, "he'll wake up and stop pretending he thinks I'm still a kid."

This puzzling behavior was soon forgotten by Sally as she and Lenore went from store to store. She was not going to let herself be extravagant and buy all the things Lenore bought. She didn't know what Mr. Andres did for a living, but whatever it was, he evidently earned far more money than her father did. Nevertheless, she was grateful to her father for allowing her to use the charge-a-plate, and she told herself she would not abuse the privilege.

When Lenore bought three or four slips or bras or panties, she bought only one or two. When Lenore bought a half-dozen pairs of stockings, she bought two pairs. And so it went with one item after another, except for phonograph records. Lenore already had many that she had wanted, so now Sally stocked up.

She was feeling so pleased with herself for resisting

many of the things Lenore bought that she picked out a new handbag and ripped off the tags so she could use it at once. It was rather expensive, but she reasoned that all the zippered pockets would be helpful in keeping her accounts straight.

"Oh, that was fun." She sighed as she sank back against the smooth upholstery of Mrs. Andres's convertible for the homeward trip.

Weejee scowled. "Sure, dames always think it's fun to spend money. They never think of the poor dope that has to pay the bills."

Lenore poked Sally and whispered, "See?"

Sally wondered just what it was that Lenore wanted her to see.

When they arrived home she took her purchases up to her room and spread them on the bed. There were more than she had realized, and after a little while her sense of pleasure began to change to dismay. The total cost was more than she had anticipated. Much more. And most of her purchases were things she didn't need. At least not right away. What she should have done, she knew now, was to figure out what she had to have before she bought anything at all.

What she wanted most of all was a new winter

coat. Her short coat, that she usually wore to school, was all right. But her other coat, the long one, just wasn't right at all.

What chance was there of getting a coat now that she'd used up practically all of her quarterly allowance?

In her dismay and disappointment she wanted to blame Lenore. If it hadn't been for Lenore buying all those frilly things she would not have been so foolish, she thought impatiently. But soon she admitted that it was not Lenore's fault. She should have had enough sense to realize that she couldn't afford all the things Lenore bought. Each item was more expensive than what she usually wore. She just hadn't used good sense, and there was nobody to blame, really, but herself.

In the days that followed she realized that not only had she frittered away her money, but she was frittering away too much time. Lenore was always wanting her to talk, or to listen to records. Lenore seemed to ignore school assignments most of the time, and so it was small wonder that her grades for the first marking period were not good.

"Oh, so what?" Lenore laughed.

But Sally could not laugh off her own grades.

Though they were much better than Lenore's, they were not what they should have been, and she was well aware of the fact without having it pointed out by her parents.

Her mother made no comment before handing Sally's report to Mr. Sorenson. Sally squirmed as she waited for someone to say something.

Finally her father said, "Do you honestly feel that this is the best you could have done, Sally?"

"Well—no," she admitted reluctantly. She tried to think of a logical reason for the letdown. "It's probably because I'm in a new school."

Neither of her parents seemed inclined to accept this.

"I'll do better next time," she assured them.

"We'll hold you to that," her father declared promptly.

She would show them, she decided. She would get really good grades in the next period.

Explaining to Lenore why she must spend more time on homework was not easy. Lenore was bright in so many ways, but some things she just could not, or would not, see. The importance of school was one of these things.

"But wouldn't you like to go to college?" Sally

asked in exasperation when once again Lenore interrupted her efforts to do her homework. "You can't, you know, unless you make good grades in high school."

"Who says I can't?" Lenore hooted. "Who's going to stop me? I guess my father can get me in—that is, if I want to go."

"Not if you flunk out before you even graduate from high school." No matter how much influence Mr. Andres had, he couldn't very well get around that.

"Oh, well, maybe I'll get married pretty soon. Maybe I'll marry Weejee."

This seemed a silly statement, yet Sally had a disturbing suspicion that Lenore might not be joking.

"At your age?" she scoffed.

"I'm almost sixteen."

Sally felt that this was one of the times when it might be important for her to say the right thing. Though Lenore often argued with her, there were times when she seemed to want Sally's opinion.

So she spoke carefully. "Even when you're sixteen, that's too soon to marry. Look how much time there is for being married. And how little time, really, for being young and single." She thought of Weejee, and she suddenly was very much concerned that Lenore might be serious about marrying Weejee, and she could think of none of the right words to describe him, except that he didn't have just the right qualities. He wasn't good or true or gentle or kind. But she dared not point this out to Lenore.

Something occurred to her, and she wondered that she had not thought of it sooner. Many boys looked at Lenore and whistled and made comments. But, as far as she knew, they didn't ask Lenore for dates.

"Lenore," she said impulsively, "I think you'd go over bigger with the kids at school if you'd try to be more like the other girls."

Lenore sat upright. Anger sparked her strange greenish-brown eyes. "What do you mean by that crack?"

"I mean," Sally said firmly, "you'd go over bigger if you'd ditch that way-out look. Be more like a high school girl and not a high-fashion model. For one thing, cut the weird-o eye makeup."

"Well, thanks, pal! Thanks for nothing," Lenore snapped, and she went home in a huff.

Sally was sorry that she had upset Lenore. Yet the more she thought about it, the more certain she was that she was right in what she'd said. Lenore's makeup was definitely not right for a high school girl. Even her hair was wrong—too bleached and unnatural looking. It was no wonder the boys whistled instead of asking for dates. Not that they were exactly falling over themselves to date *her,* Sally thought glumly.

Now that she knew she was going to have to wear her old coat for a while, it seemed to get more impossible every day. She talked about getting a part-time job.

"If I were sixteen I could make about a dollar and a half an hour as a checker and bagger at one of the supermarkets, after school and on Saturday," she thought.

With Christmas drawing close, she needed money for presents. Jonni's mother was spending more time at their book shop, and even Jonni sometimes went there to help.

"I wish we had a store," she told her parents. "Then I could work there and earn some extra money."

"Just so it's not a food store," her father said, teasing. "You and Lu, between you, would probably eat up the profits."

Then one day Mrs. Sorenson said if Sally really wanted a job, she could work at home and get paid for doing it.

"I've been asked to assist the new woman who is in charge of scheduling and grades at your school," she said with a pleased smile. "If you girls think you can lend a hand with the housework so I won't be bogged down with carrying two jobs, I'll tell Mr. Hardie I accept."

Sally had mixed emotions about having her mother in the office at school. Somehow it didn't seem quite the same now as when she was younger, to have her mother at school. Still, she did want to earn some money. Housework wouldn't be quite so bad, she was sure, if she got paid for doing it.

She wanted to tell someone. Right away. So she walked over to Lenore's, even though Lenore had not been very cordial recently. When she rang the bell she thought she heard voices raised in anger. More than once she had overheard Lenore's parents quarreling. And Lenore's mother screamed at Lenore sometimes, and at the boys.

These indications of family friction always upset Sally, and she was about to turn away. But Lenore was already at the door, and she pulled Sally by the hand to her bedroom with its white furniture and turquoise blue carpeting and cushions.

"Sit there," she said, motioning toward the chaise

longue. "Diana and Gus are arguing again. Don't mind them."

To Sally it seemed disrespectful of Lenore to refer to her parents by their first names, but she forgot that as she told Lenore her news.

Lenore looked puzzled. "But why do you want to do more housework? You already have to do so many things." At Lenore's, a couple came in to do most of the work.

"To earn some money," Sally answered honestly.

This seemed to mean nothing to Lenore. "You're always busy now with studying. There won't be any time at all for us to have fun if you're going to be the family scrub lady," she said crossly.

So now she was the scrub lady! Lenore was always putting tags on people, and now she'd put a tag on her, and she didn't like it. She wasn't at all sure that she liked Lenore. In fact, she was quite sure she did not.

"If it hadn't been for you," Sally said in a burst of anger, "I probably wouldn't have charged so much stuff and I'd have the coat I need. And now when I'm trying to earn money because I need it, you make nasty remarks."

"I never made nasty remarks," Lenore declared

virtuously. "You're touchy, that's what you are. You just can't take it."

"You did so! And I'm not!" Sally insisted, heading for the door.

She hurried home to her own room where nobody would see her tears. She no longer had a friend who understood her. Everything was changed, without Sue. Everything was so muddled. And she had never been so miserable in her whole life.

15

Dream Gift

Her friendship with Lenore was over, Sally was sure. She couldn't blame Lenore for being huffy. Now that she'd had time to think about it, she realized that what she'd said to Lenore had been entirely uncalled for. Why had she tried to pin the blame on Lenore for something she knew very well was her own fault?

She told herself it was just as well that she and Lenore had come to the parting of the ways. Now she would have more time for Jonni. Jonni was superior to Lenore in so many ways. She was so understanding, for one thing. Even when she had neglected to tell Jonni that she would not be going to her home for "mustgos," Jonni had not been angry.

She was the one who had been embarrassed about the whole thing. If she hadn't felt ashamed of herself, she might have given more time to Jonni, regardless of Lenore.

Now she would have time for Jonni. But Jonni was busy these days, she remembered. Jonni might not have any time for her, except for snatches during school hours, until the holiday sales season was over.

There were things about Lenore that she would miss. Lenore was fun to be with. There were always things to laugh about when Lenore was around. She was like Sue in that respect. Sally realized for the first time that they both liked to poke fun at other people. Could this be a sign of uncertainty on their part? She wondered about this. There were some people who tore others down in order to build themselves up, she supposed.

She could not accept this as applying to either Lenore or Sue. They both had plenty of self-confidence, that she knew.

In the morning she dawdled over leaving for school, trying not to think how it would be without Lenore.

Long ago her mother had said it wasn't wise to depend too much on just one person for friendship. Maybe it had been a mistake to spend so much of her time with Lenore. And even with Sue. Maybe her mother had been right.

To her surprise, Lenore, who never liked to wait for anyone, was waiting for her on the walk at the side of the house. For a moment Sally was so pleased, and even touched, that she dared not speak.

Then she said, "Hi," as if she had not for a moment doubted that Lenore would be there—as if she had not been certain that Lenore would be too proud to make a move to end their quarrel, if it could be called a quarrel.

She said quickly, "I'm sorry about yesterday, Lenore."

Lenore looked startled. "For what?"

"I shouldn't have said those things to you," Sally admitted, relieved to get it off her conscience. "It wasn't your fault that I spent too much money that day. I really knew that all the time."

"Skip it," Lenore insisted. "Let's talk about something more interesting."

Perhaps Lenore did not take quarrels too seriously, Sally reasoned, remembering the many angry words overheard at Lenore's house. Moreover, in all this time she had never met Lenore's father; she had only seen him coming and going in his big black limousine. But she had heard him, bellowing in anger.

Thinking of this, for just a moment she was gratefully aware of her own family. At times she felt that her parents expected too much from her. At times they had differences of opinion. But they never yelled or screamed at each other, the way Lenore's family did.

With Christmas drawing close, she was more aware than ever of both family and friends. There were many gifts to buy and wrap. She felt a little sad when she remembered how she and Sue always made such a big secret of what they would give each other.

There would be no present from Sue this year, she guessed. But when she was doing her Christmas shopping she saw a bright green clutch purse that seemed just right for Sue. So she wrapped it in her best holiday wrappings and put it aside just in case, and without a card.

The money for doing extra work around the house, added to her usual Christmas Club savings account, made her feel almost wealthy for a little while. But she was determined to spend her money sensibly from now on, and to build up enough reserve for the coat she wanted. So her gifts for the family were both inexpensive and practical. And she asked for the same in return.

Early on Christmas morning they gathered about the Christmas tree, as was their custom, and sang carols as they opened the many packages. Sally saw that her request had been granted. Each of her presents was something practical. Things to wear. Things for school. Things she needed. This was what she insisted she wanted, and yet it was somehow disappointing not to have one person disregard her instructions. Even the leather gloves from her sister Linda were fleece-lined for warmth.

Only the holiday dinner promised to be just what it should be. She was in the kitchen, trying to hurry everything along, when Lenore appeared bearing a large package that seemed even larger because of the glitter of bows and wrapping paper.

Lucia looked up from the wooden bowl in which she was chopping giblets for the gravy. "Jumping jelly beans!" she exclaimed. "You should get a prize for the sparklingest gift wrapping, Lenore."

Smiling, Lenore held the big box toward Sally. "For you."

In her momentary dismay, Sally almost said, "But I haven't anything for you!"

She should have known, she told herself reproachfully. Knowing Lenore, she should have known Lenore would have a gift for her. Then she remembered the package she had wrapped so carefully. It had no card on it.

"Lu," she coaxed, "would you run up and get the package that's on my dresser?"

"Well—it's Christmas," Lu said cheerfully, and she went bounding up the stairs.

Sally led Lenore to the living room where the opened packages had been piled under the tree. Lenore had already seen the tree, but now she remarked, "It's the real old-fashioned kind. All red and green, except the angels and tinsel."

Sally didn't know how to answer this. At Lenore's house floodlights had been shining on two huge pink trees for several weeks.

She managed to slide a box out of all the fancy coverings. On the box was the imprint of the Flair Shop, the expensive shop where Lenore bought so many things. In the box was something diaphanous, something heavenly blue.

"Oh, what a beautiful color," Sally breathed,

scarcely daring to lift the billows from the box.

There were two garments, she discovered. A nightgown, and a peignoir to match.

"It's like something out of a dream." Then Sally bit her lip to steady it as the thought struck her that her mother would probably make her give this back. She was sure she couldn't bear it if she were not allowed to keep Lenore's gift. She had never owned anything like this. Actually she had never before had any particular desire to own anything like this. But her gifts had all been so practical this Christmas, she was sure it would be unbearably painful to part with this lovely present.

Her mother had come into the room and was eyeing the billows of blue with doubt written plainly on her face.

"Oh, Mother!" Sally cried pleadingly. "It's the most beautiful—I've never had anything like this—" She said again, "It's like something out of a dream."

Lenore had torn the wrappings from the green clutch purse. "Your gift is lovely, too," she said, as if she really found the small purse pleasing.

Mrs. Sorenson said, "I don't want to be a spoilsport, Lenore, especially at Christmas. But did your mother approve your giving this to Sally?"

"Of course," Lenore answered promptly. "She even helped me pick it out."

Sally saw that this was perplexing to her mother. And no wonder. For Mrs. Andres accepted no invitations and she rejected every effort of the neighbors to be friendly.

Still looking uncertain, Mrs. Sorenson said, "In that case you may keep it, Sally, though I hope that if you girls exchange gifts in the future, they will be inexpensive ones. It really is better that way."

Sally was ecstatic. She couldn't seem to get enough of examining her gift from Lenore, holding it up, putting it carefully back in the box. It wasn't that she wanted to wear it, really. It was the beauty of it, the thought of something so lovely belonging to her, that was so thrilling.

Lucia did not understand this. "You can't wear it," Lucia pointed out. "Not where anybody can see it—because they'd see you, right through that thing. So what good is it?"

There were other times when Sally found her sister trying. According to the agreement with their mother, Lucia also had extra household chores these days, for which she, too, received extra money. This money went into her "pony bank." She had not given up her hope of having a horse of her own. Now that snow covered the ground she could not ride her beloved "Horace" out-of-doors, but several times during the Christmas holidays she rode her bike in the basement, and now and then startling whoops sounded from down below.

Mrs. Sorenson defended Lucia's actions. "She doesn't have anyone to play with just now. Peggy and Debbie have colds, and I'd rather she didn't go too far from home in this weather. Even Lenore's brothers aren't around these days to tease her."

The two boys and Lenore had gone to Florida with their mother, as Sally very well knew. Lenore had said, "Why don't you come with us?" Just as if all a girl had to do was decide and then pack a suitcase. As if a person didn't ever have to think about things like money.

One morning, shortly before the holidays ended, Lucia slept unusually late, and when she came downstairs in her woolly pink pajamas Sally said, "You might as well eat now."

She was in charge. Her father was at work. Her mother had an appointment with the dentist.

Lu looked cute in those pajamas, Sally thought—cute and sort of babyish, with her hair all flyaway about her face and her eyes still full of sleep.

To show that she had not forgotten her mother's rules about dressing for meals, Sally said, "If you don't eat now, it will be lunchtime before you get your breakfast."

Lu yawned hugely as she poured milk over her cereal. "It was those men again," she said sleepily.

"What men?" Sally asked, thinking with amusement that Lu was still in a dream world.

"The ones that go into the carriage house at night." Lu dipped into the cereal bowl. "I was watching them."

Sally felt it her duty to speak firmly to her sister. "Don't you know it's not nice to be a snooper, watching to see what other people are doing?"

"I wasn't snooping." Lu defended herself. "They were noisy last night, and they woke me up. First somebody laughed. Loud. Then somebody talked. Even louder. I heard a man say, 'Shut up, you fool! You want the cops on us?' Then they went into the carriage house, but I couldn't go to sleep for a long time."

She paused before spooning cereal into her mouth. "Why would they think the cops would be after them, Sally?" she asked.

"You were dreaming," Sally said quickly.

This did not convince Lucia, and Sally was not sure that she herself was convinced. Thoughtfully she added, "If somebody said it, he might have meant they were being too noisy for that time of night and one of the neighbors might complain to the police. Doesn't that make sense?"

"I suppose so," Lu admitted.

Sally went on, making an effort to be patient with Lu, "Apparently Mr. Andres uses some place in the carriage house as a kind of extra office, the way Daddy uses our den." She thought of something else. "Mrs. Andres probably doesn't want a lot of people tramping in and out of her house, dirtying her white carpeting."

"I guess so," Lu said, and Sally wanted to shake her, because she still did not look convinced.

Getting back to school was a relief. Lenore had not yet returned from Florida, but it was good to see Jonni.

"I never knew so many people wanted to exchange the books they got for Christmas." Jonni laughed. "After the Christmas rush the stocks are low, and we were busy trying to get the customer what he wanted."

Obviously Jonni had enjoyed working in her father's store. Jonni also had gone to some holiday parties in her neighborhood. Sally felt left out, thinking how unusually quiet her days had been.

A day or two later, she and Jonni were together in the hall after school when Judd and Myron blocked their way to ask if they were going to the next school "mixer." She and Sue had gone to mixers in their freshman year. In fact, she and Sue used to have plenty of things to do and places to go. She had been missing out on fun, Sally decided, partly because of wanting to be faithful to the old school, and partly because of Lenore. Lenore turned up her nose at so many things. And so they had missed out on fun.

"I'd like to go," she told the boys. Let them take that however they pleased.

"Good!" Myron said.

Judd said, "Swell!"

Jonni said, "I want to go, too."

They all laughed.

"Then it's a date," Judd said. "We'll all go together."

Lenore returned home before the mixer. Sally told her, "You can go with us, Lenore. Mixers are for everybody, you know, not just couples."

Some boys were sure to ask Lenore to dance. Some of the boys who were always looking at her, and whistling.

At first Lenore was not going to "a silly old pop and cookies party," as she called it. But she changed her mind. Just why, Sally didn't know. Though she felt ashamed of herself because of it, Sally had rather hoped Lenore would not go with them. Things would be considerably more relaxed without Lenore. Besides, Lenore didn't like Myron. She was always making fun of him.

But on the night of the party she didn't make fun of him. She even arranged for her mother to drive them all, and the only thing she said about Myron's height was, "Myron has gone out for the basketball team, Mother. They need tall boys for the team."

"That's nice," Mrs. Andres said. She smiled all the way to the school building, as if she found the whole thing very amusing—as if she couldn't wait to tell her friends, whoever they might be, "It was a scream. Just a scream!" Though just what was so funny about taking a carful of kids to a school party, Sally couldn't imagine.

Lenore had a Florida tan that made her stand out even more than usual. Her dress was pale green and her eye makeup matched the color of her dress perfectly.

Sally was so busy enjoying herself, dancing with Judd and Myron and even with a few other boys, that it didn't dawn on her until the party was almost over that Lenore's partners were, for the most part, the loudest, brashest boys in school—the ones most of the girls tried to avoid. If she hadn't known Lenore, Sally would have thought Lenore didn't mind. But she knew her just well enough to suspect the reason why Lenore was talking so much. Lenore was trying not to let anyone know that she minded.

It was time for the last dance, and Sally whispered to Myron, "Ask Lenore. Please?"

He made a face, but he asked Lenore. She supposed Judd had already asked Jonni. Then she saw that Jonni had been asked by a boy named Ted Olsen, who lived on her street. And, though it seemed almost a miracle, Judd was waiting to ask her for the last dance.

She liked Judd. He wasn't as handsome as Whit Fowler, of course. And he was not exactly an expert dancer. But neither was she, though Judd made her feel like an expert. And that wasn't all. He also made her feel pretty and important. She wondered how much he liked Jonni, and how much Jonni liked him. Then she forgot that as she savored the music and the fun of dancing and the pleasure of having the last dance with Judd.

"It's been a swell party," Judd said as the music stopped.

"Oh, yes!" she agreed.

Before Mrs. Andres arrived with the white convertible, Jonni and Judd decided to walk home.

"It's such a beautiful night," Jonni said in explanation.

The night *was* beautiful, with a star-spangled sky and the air all crisp and clean. Sally tried not to wonder if Jonni was walking because of the beauty of the night or because she wanted to be alone with Judd.

She scarcely heard Lenore say in a low tone, "Maybe you were right, Sally."

"Wh—what?" she stammered, wondering if Lenore had somehow read her thoughts.

"Maybe," Lenore admitted, "I shouldn't use so much makeup. Maybe the boys don't go for stuff like that."

"Oh—maybe," she answered, reluctant to think of anyone else's problems at this moment.

She wanted to think about Judd. About dancing

Lenore looked at him with a kind of awe. And Myron no longer seemed so awkward; or, if so, it was an endearing awkwardness.

As for Myron himself, he was frankly enjoying his sudden popularity; but he was not at all puffed up about it. On the contrary, he insisted, "Today's hero is tomorrow's bum. If you help to win the game you're a hero. If you help to lose it you're a bum, and people forget you in a hurry."

"That sounds cruel," Sally protested.

"But it's true," Lenore agreed matter-of-factly.

She went to the games with Sally and Jonni. Judd went with them if the game was on a night when he didn't have to work. Judd had several part-time jobs, and though Sally admired him for this, she often found it disappointing when Judd was not available. Having a boy at hand could be very pleasant, and of course Myron couldn't sit with them at the games. She wasn't sure these days which one she liked better, Judd or Myron.

When it was time for their team to play the old school, Sally was filled with mixed emotions. This much she knew: She wanted Myron to do his very best. And she also wanted Hadley East to see him doing his best. This, she knew, was in keeping with the philosophy he'd stated on that day in the kitchen—her "kitchen date"—when they had all discussed school loyalty. His idea of playing the game was to beat his own past record, and he felt the same about his team.

Remembering the thrill of hearing the cheerleaders at the football game use the words she'd written, she decided to write a cheer especially for Myron, and she found that it almost wrote itself.

My, my, my, my!
Myron! Myron!
Hadley!
Wes-s-s-t!

The game was to be held at the old school, and as the date drew closer, she wondered if she could bear to go.

Myron's parents were going to the game, and they offered to take Sally and Lenore and Jonni in their car. Mr. and Mrs. Burdick never seemed at a loss for the right things to say. Both were tall and handsome. In a few years Myron would probably look like them, Sally decided, and that was not bad.

To her amazement Mrs. Burdick said, "We've been wanting to tell you, Sally, how grateful we are to you for getting Myron interested in basketball."

"Me?" she said incredulously.

"For a while he was so wrapped up in his music," Mrs. Burdick explained, "he just couldn't see the need for much else. We tried to convince him that it sometimes is not wise to neglect other opportunities. But he couldn't seem to see it—until you encouraged him to go out for basketball again. He did play a little in seventh grade, you know, but we thought he'd given up athletics for good."

Sally was dumbfounded. They were giving her credit for something she was sure she didn't deserve. If she protested it would probably sound like false modesty. She didn't know what to say, except, "Oh, but I don't deserve any credit. It was just one of those things."

As they walked into her old school, she was still thinking how amazing it was, and rather wonderful, that she should have had a part in making a star of Myron.

"You girls go along," Mr. Burdick said with a big smile, "and have fun. We'll meet you here when the game is over."

Sally scarcely heard him. She was in her beloved Hadley. The original Hadley. It hadn't changed. The same narrow hallways. The same echoing noises of voices and footsteps on the stairways. How many times she had climbed those stairs! And there was the door leading to the auditorium. The door was closed, but she could picture the rows on rows of seats, their curved backs marred by students' pencilings and carvings. She could envision the dark folds of velveteen drapes on the shallow stage. All very old-fashioned compared with Hadley East.

As they moved toward the gymnasium to take their places among the eager spectators, she was uncomfortably aware that this was the school that *used* to be her school. Coming back was very like returning for a visit to the junior high building—just as Myron had said it should be. There were fond memories, but no heartbreak.

She felt let down, unhappy with herself. Surely she lacked strength of character if her sense of loyalty was no stronger than this? Surely she should stand by her old love, regardless?

Just then she saw Sue coming toward them. Sue was with Whit and another boy and girl. Sally froze with uncertainty. She didn't know what to say or if she should say anything at all. For she and Sue had not spoken a single word to each other since that awful day when she had had to break the news to Sue concerning Whit.

It was Whit who spoke first, saying pleasantly, "How've you been, Sally? Long time no see you know who, as Confucius would say. Or would Confucius say *whom?*"

Sally said, "Hi," and she managed a smile.

Then Sue said, "Hi," in a cool way quite unlike her usual breezy manner. And, very properly, she introduced Ann Ainsley and her brother Lester. Sally presented Lenore and Jonni, and also Judd, who had suddenly appeared at their heels.

Though she had been fully prepared to dislike Ann Ainsley, Sally was aware of the girl's charm and warm sincerity.

"Sue and Whit have mentioned you so often," Ann said. "I was beginning to wonder if we weren't ever going to meet."

It was just as wrong, Sally told herself chidingly, to decide against someone just because that person happened to have money, as it was to judge someone because of not having money. Ann Ainsley deserved to be judged for herself. Sally was particularly impressed with Ann's ease of manner with Judd, and the way she let him know that she recognized his name in connection with the false accusations against him.

It occurred to her that Whit might show at least a small amount of embarrassment at facing Judd. After all, Judd had been blamed for something Whit had done. Instead, Whit was paying special attention to Lenore. She couldn't find it in her heart to blame anyone for paying attention to Lenore, now that Lenore had stopped using too much makeup and let her own natural prettiness show.

The two groups parted, but not before Whit called, "Sure you wouldn't rather sit on our side, Sally?"

He was making a joke, of course. But she wasn't sure just which side she wanted to sit on. Not until the game was over did she know. Not until after she had ecstatically joined the others in shouting, "My, my, my, my!" for Myron, and for Hadley West. The team—*her* team—maneuvered the ball into scoring position and Myron shot it into the basket with clocklike efficiency for point after point.

Even so, Hadley West did not make enough points—not enough to defeat the old school. The old school won, by a score of sixty to fifty-three.

Smarting though she was with the sting of defeat, Sally now knew for sure that, win or lose, Hadley West was her school.

On the way out of the building she saw Sue again, and Whit and the Ainsleys.

Whit stopped to whisper to the girls, "I won a little money on the game. Wouldn't you like to help me spend it?"

Hearing Whit speak of gambling was even more upsetting than losing the game. Sally saw that Lenore stepped quickly away from Whit, as if she, too, found it disturbing to hear Whit talk this way. Whit apparently hadn't learned his lesson. Maybe the police had been too easy on him.

Whit, Sally decided unhappily, was continuing to get involved with the wrong things.

17

The Law Moves In

Sally saw the very coat she wanted on a mannikin in a store window. It was a lovely shade of red, and it had a black pile lining and a detachable hood. It was marked down, and what if someone should buy it before she could? The store was a small one, in the local shopping area, and not one where she could use her mother's charge-a-plate.

The saleswoman said, "We could put it on lay-away for you, if you'd like to make a small deposit."

Even counting every penny in her purse, she didn't

have as much as the saleswoman asked for.

"I guess it will be all right," the woman said with an understanding smile. "The coat does seem to belong to you."

Sally agreed wholeheartedly. It was her coat. She just had to have it.

It didn't matter that, having given the saleswoman all her money, she had to walk more than a mile against a cold wind instead of taking the bus. All that mattered now was the problem of convincing her parents that she had done the right thing.

She was glad they were both at home when she got there, so she could face them at once.

As she told them, she tried to read their verdict from the look on their faces, but could not.

She went on to point out how much she needed the new coat, and what a bargain she was getting. She also promised to do whatever they wanted her to do, if only she could have the coat.

Her mother said, "It's late in the season, but often that's the time to get a bargain. If you are sure you won't tire of red?"

"Oh, not this red," Sally assured her. "I'd never tire of this red."

In that case, her father said, there remained the

matter of paying for the coat. "That could be arranged, of course, if we felt reasonably certain that you would live up to your part of the bargain. From what I've seen and heard, Sally, I'm afraid you haven't been as faithful as you might about doing the things your mother is paying you to do around the house."

Her mother said, "And there's also your schoolwork. This last report was better, but not as good as it might have been. And it would probably be a favor to Lenore if you didn't spend so much time with her. She needs more study time, too."

For just a moment she was envious of Lenore. She was sure Lenore never had to go through anything like this just to get a new coat.

But honesty compelled her to admit, "I guess you're right. I get involved with Lenore—and talking on the phone with her and with Jonni—and I don't get at the housework as soon as I should."

Thinking of the beautiful red coat, she was willing to agree to almost anything, especially after her parents said she might as well have it right away so she could be wearing it during the remainder of the cold weather.

It was not easy to convince Lenore that changes had to be made. Lenore came over after school, even though Sally had tried to explain that she would be busy.

"I guess I'll have to ask you to go home," Sally said, embarrassed at having to be so blunt about it. "My parents let me get the coat, and I've got to live up to my part of the bargain."

Lenore looked more unhappy than Sally had ever seen her. At last she confessed, "I know I should spend more time on schoolwork, Sally. But there's just no place at our house that's right for studying. And nobody cooperates. The radio or the television or the hi-fi is blasting all day long. Not to mention the little monsters and their perpetual racket."

After pondering all this, Sally suggested, "Why don't you study in the carriage house?"

Lenore turned her head away abruptly. Then, as if to change the subject, she admitted, "This year I didn't try very hard in school. I thought I didn't have to. Then when I got behind and knew I should catch up, I just didn't know how. I can't seem to get back on the track."

She looked at Sally pleadingly. "You could help me, Sally. You could help me catch up. I don't want to flunk."

Sally didn't want her to flunk. Yet she didn't see

how she could possibly help Lenore in addition to the work she'd promised to do around the house and her own school assignments as well. Because Lenore looked so unhappy she said, "I'll see if I can think of something."

What she really meant was that she would ask her parents for suggestions. The more she thought about it, the more certain she was that there was nothing she could do.

So she was not very happy when her mother said, "You could probably help her all right, Sally, if you are willing to make the sacrifice."

"Sacrifice!" Sally yelped. "I should think it would be a sacrifice! Why, I don't even know how I'm going to do all I have to do already—without taking on Lenore besides!"

Mrs. Sorenson did not argue the point. Instead she said, "Lenore's rating in comprehension tests is high. So it certainly isn't that she's not capable of doing good work. Apparently her parents just don't realize that the school can't do it all."

Lenore had said, "Nobody cooperates."

It would do no good to try to talk to Lenore's parents. When Royal and Junior, from time to time, got into trouble at school, Mrs. Andres went to the school and made a scene, blaming the teachers and the principal and everyone but Royal and Junior. No, it was not very likely that Lenore would get any help at home.

So, though she didn't want to, Sally told Lenore she would try to help her.

"But it's got to be strictly business," Sally warned. "I have things besides schoolwork to do, things that must be done."

When Lenore came for help, Sally went from household tasks to her own homework to Lenore's. Sometimes they used the kitchen table as their desk. And sometimes they shared Sally's little desk.

Lenore said one day, "I really love this desk. And I love your furniture and everything about your house. But best of all I love your room. I guess because some of the furniture is from your ancestors. It sort of shows you loved them, and they loved you."

Amazement tied Sally's tongue. She had been feeling cross with Lenore, and now she was ashamed. She had not dreamed that Lenore admired her furniture. On the contrary, she had supposed that to Lenore all these old things would seem ugly.

She had been cross with Lenore because of Whit. Ever since the night of the basketball game at Hadley

East, Whit and Corny had been hanging around Lenore's house. According to Lucia, even when Lenore was not home the two boys hung around.

"They even poke around the carriage house," Lucia insisted.

Sally was just about convinced that the carriage house was becoming an obsession with her sister. As for Whit and Corny hanging around, she tried not to be jealous of Whit's interest in Lenore. But jealousy apparently wasn't something that would go away just because she wanted it to.

So she made more effort than ever to help Lenore with her schoolwork, and, as if in reward, one day Lenore said, "I wish that old Whit Fowler and his friend Corny would stay over on their own street."

Sally laughed aloud in her relief. "You don't like them?"

Lenore shrugged. "I don't dislike them exactly. But Weejee is getting a little burned at them for being around all the time."

Sally sobered. "Do you still like Weejee?" she asked anxiously.

She didn't want Lenore to be too fond of Whit. But, even more, she didn't want her to be fond of Weejee. Lenore certainly deserved someone better than Weejee, of this much she was sure.

A snort of contempt accompanied Lenore's answer. "That creep? Weejee? Who needs him?"

Sally was so relieved, she couldn't bear to sit still. "Come on downstairs," she said. "It's time for refreshments. You've earned a break."

The next morning Lucia was late in coming down for breakfast. She insisted that something had been going on at the carriage house the night before which had kept her awake.

"Oh, not that again!" Sally moaned.

"But it's true," Lucia insisted. "There were bright lights flashing, and men all over the place—some looked like policemen—and they took things out of the carriage house before they went away—"

Sally rose from the table impatiently. "I don't have time for fairy tales this morning."

One of her Thursday morning chores was stripping the sheets and pillowcases from her bed. Now, while she was replacing them with clean ones, she discovered that her dark wool skirt was liberally covered with lint. By the time she had given the skirt a thorough brushing, a look at the clock sent her scurrying down the stairs.

Lenore was not in sight. Sally dared not wait, for

she had barely enough time to make it to school.

All day she had the feeling that there was news of some sort making the rounds, but nobody told her what it was. Nobody joined her as she walked home, and she missed Lenore.

When she picked up the local paper from the porch stairs to carry it into the house, she knew why Lenore was not in school. And now she knew that Lucia had been right all along about the carriage house.

There actually had been men going in and out of the carriage house the night before. And there had been lights flashing. For the carriage house had been raided by law enforcement officers, and Mr. Andres had been arrested and charged with illegal possession of slot machines and other gambling paraphernalia. According to the news story, the gambling machines had been transported across state lines, which was a federal offense. So Mr. Andres was being charged with breaking federal as well as local laws.

Sally had meant to give the front page a mere glance before telephoning Lenore to ask why she had not been in school. Now she could not phone Lenore, even if Lenore should want her to, and she was certain Lenore would not want anyone phoning her right now.

Not now, with the story all over the front page of the *Linden Leader*. Everyone would know now where Mr. Andres got all the money that Lenore spent so freely. And where the money came from that paid for the two big automobiles. And for all the trips, and the fine clothes, and the house with its beautiful furnishings. Lenore's father, according to the paper, was connected with a gambling syndicate which was active in Linden.

Sally unbuttoned her coat, but she forgot to remove it as she became engrossed in the story in an adjoining column.

Efforts had been going on for some time, the story stated, to catch those who were responsible for the gambling that had been taking place at school athletic events in the county. Parlay cards had shown up at game after game, and finally the aid of several high school boys had been enlisted by local law officials. These boys, the paper stated, deserved much of the credit for the successful timing of the raid, which was made before the parlay cards and other evidence were removed from the premises. Without them, the raid could not have been staged.

Boys, Sally thought. Which boys? Whit? And Corny? Was that why Whit had been hanging around

Lenore's house these past few weeks?

Sue would know. Though Sally had not phoned Sue in a very long while, she knew that today she just had to phone her.

18

Lines Are Busy

Three times she got the busy signal. On the fourth try Sue answered.

Sue was ecstatic. "Sally, how nice of you to call! I suppose you heard the big news?"

"Yes, I heard," Sally said. "Rather, I read it. And of course I wondered if Whit was one of the—"

Sally interrupted, her words spilling over with happiness. "He certainly was one of the boys they mentioned in the paper. Isn't it wonderful, Sally? Now Whit's a hero. This makes up for the other thing. I think they should have mentioned his name in the paper. But I guess they didn't this time because they didn't the other time. But I think everyone should know how Whit stuck to his guns—"

Sue giggled over her own choice of words. "Whit didn't have any guns, of course. But he did just what the police asked him to do. They asked Whit and Corny if they would like to make up for that other thing. Of course they said yes. And they were the ones who set up the raid that got Mr. Andres arrested. Isn't it exciting, Sally?"

Sally agreed that it was exciting, even as she wondered how Lenore was taking all this. Lenore must have known all along. That was why Lenore seldom wanted to go to the school games. And probably why Weejee went; he undoubtedly had some connection with the parlay cards. And now she knew why Lenore acted strangely whenever the carriage house was mentioned.

"Poor Lenore!" Sally said. "This is going to be pretty rough on her."

Sue did not agree. "She probably doesn't care at all. Maybe she even likes the publicity."

"Oh, you don't know Lenore! Besides, it isn't her fault, what her father has done."

Sue wanted to talk of other things. "One wonderful thing about all this is that Whit is getting that new car, after all. Daddy is proud of what Whit did, and he's sure there will be no more of that other nonsense."

"Oh, I'm glad," Sally said. She meant she was glad Whit was to have his car. She hoped Sue and Mr. Fowler were right in thinking there would be no more of "that other nonsense" from Whit. She sincerely hoped he had learned his lesson.

She was disturbed because Sue seemed so heartless toward Lenore. In a way Whit had been heartless, too, pretending to be interested in Lenore. But, she decided, Whit had been on an important mission, and he really couldn't help that innocent persons might be hurt along with the guilty ones.

Sue said in a burst of laughter, "I suppose you know who was Whit's chief informer?"

"No. Who?"

"Your sister. Lu."

Sally found it hard to believe that her little sister could have informed Whit of anything.

"Things she said cinched their suspicions—things about that remodeled old barn. The carriage house, Whit said she always called it."

Sally felt a little sick. If she had paid attention to the things Lu had been saying all along about the carriage house, was it possible that she might have kept some of this from happening? Not that she wanted Mr. Andres to escape punishment. If he had been breaking the law, he deserved to be punished. It was Lenore Sally was thinking about. But why should she think she could keep Lenore from being hurt? Wasn't it bound to happen, her father being what he was?

Sue said, "I guess we won't be seeing much of the white convertible girl after this. What about the horse girl?"

"Her name is Jonni," Sally said defensively, even as she decided that it was not necessary to defend Jonni. When Sue got to know Jonni, she would see that.

Still in the bubbly way that Sally had always admired so much, Sue ended the conversation by saying, "We'll have to get together real quick-like, Sally, and talk some more about all these exciting things that are going on in our town."

"Yes," Sally agreed, "we'll have to do that."

Wasn't this what she'd been wanting, and missing, all these months—talking with Sue? Why then, she wondered, did she feel so let down?

No sooner had she put the phone back in its place

in the upstairs alcove, than Jonni phoned to say her mother had just called her attention to the newspaper story about Lenore's father.

"How perfectly awful for Lenore," Jonni said sympathetically. "She'll need friends to stand by her. Someone should go to see her, or call her up, but I don't feel that I'm the one to do it. She might think I was intruding."

It was obvious to Sally that Jonni thought she should be the one to contact Lenore. She didn't want to do it. The mere thought of it upset her. But she agreed with Jonni that they must stand by Lenore. Regardless of what anyone, including Sue, might think.

As she had suspected they might, her parents agreed with Jonni. She should do it. But she put it off.

"About now," Mrs. Sorenson said after the dinner dishes were washed, "Lenore is probably thinking she hasn't a friend in the world."

Sally tried to imagine what she would be thinking if she were in Lenore's place, and that gave her the courage to dial Lenore's number.

One of the boys answered. "I suppose you saw all that stuff about us in the paper," he said, sounding brash as ever, as if the news stories were something to be proud of.

Royal and Junior would probably never change; they would probably always be little monsters, she decided as the boy yelled to Lenore to come to the phone.

Lenore spoke uncertainly. "Sally?" she said, as if she could not quite believe it.

Sally pretended not to notice that Lenore's voice was thick with tears. She said, as if this were just any day, that she'd missed Lenore that morning.

"And I'll have you know I was almost late," she said accusingly, "because of waiting for you."

It was not strictly true that she had waited, but she wanted to say what she might have said on any normal day.

Lenore gulped. "Don't you know, Sally? Haven't you heard?"

She answered as calmly as possible. "About your father? Yes, I heard. And I read about it. I guess most everyone has, or will. But you still have to go to school, you know. What your father did or didn't do doesn't count as an excuse for missing school."

Lenore burst into tears. After a while she said, "Sally, you're—you're the best friend—I can't tell you. And I appreciate it. But, Sally, I can't possibly face everyone at school."

"Sure you can," Sally insisted, managing somehow to hold her voice firm. "It will be like first day in a new school all over again. Only now you have friends."

As Lenore started to sob again, Sally hastened to tell her that Jonni expected to see Lenore in school the next day.

"Besides," Sally joked, "I don't want all my hard work to go to waste—all that teachering."

That was what Lenore had called Sally's tutoring —"teachering."

This brought a feeble snicker from Lenore. After a while she said, "I'm glad I didn't fall for that witless Whit, or his corny friend, Corny."

In her relief at having the conversation going so well, this struck Sally as enormously funny, and she could not stop laughing, especially after Lenore started to laugh with her.

19

Never the Same

Lenore did not go back to school until Monday. Mrs. Sorenson said, "It's probably better this way. Everyone has had time to calm down a little and stop talking so much."

Sally agreed. Over the weekend she had had time to think things over carefully. Although she sometimes found parental advice a little hard to bear, especially if her parents talked on for very long, this was one time when she was glad to hear what they had to say about the matter.

It all seemed to be summed up when her father declared, "No matter how much we may sympathize with Lenore and want to help her, this doesn't change the facts about her father. He not only broke the law, but his activities encouraged young people to break the law also. What's more, gambling can become an addiction. The addicts are forever trying to get something for nothing. And in the long run they always end up getting nothing for something."

As for Lenore, Mr. and Mrs. Sorenson agreed that Sally must go on helping with her schoolwork, and also try to be a good friend at a time when Lenore certainly needed friends.

When the two girls were alone together, either out-of-doors or in the Sorenson home, it was easy to forget about Mr. Andres, who had been released from police custody on bail. At school it was not so easy to forget that Lenore was the daughter of a man who might be sent to prison. But Lenore showed a courage that surprised Sally. Also, she became even more earnest about her schoolwork, and the teachers went out of their way to help her.

On a Saturday morning Sue dropped in to see Sally. It was so like old times, having Sue sitting tailor-fashion on the bed, that Sally choked up with happiness.

And, to add to her delight, she saw that Sue was wearing the little owl pin, the twin to her own, that symbolized undying friendship.

Sue was overflowing with conversation. She mentioned Lenore. To Sally's relief, she seemed pleased to hear that Lenore was doing so well. But mostly Sue talked about Ann Ainsley, and Ann's brother Lester, and her other new friends.

When it was time for Sue to leave, Sally walked halfway with her, as they had done so many times during the years of their friendship. It was a pleasant day, with a welcome hint of spring in the air.

By the next Saturday the wind was blowing cold again. When Lenore rang the doorbell Sally stared in surprise. Lenore was wearing a smart wool walking suit, which Sally had seen before. But she was also wearing a hat and gloves, and Sally sensed that she came bearing serious tidings.

"I can't stay," Lenore said. "We just came from the city, and I wanted to tell you the big news, Sally. We'll be moving soon, and I'll be going to a boarding school."

"Boarding school," Sally repeated wonderingly. She had never known anyone who went to a boarding school. She was impressed.

"It's a good school," Lenore said earnestly. "A really good school. They'd never have accepted me if it hadn't been for you—for your teachering."

They smiled together a little at that, though Sally felt close to tears. She knew she would miss Lenore. In that moment she felt closer to Lenore than to any girl she had ever known. They had laughed together. And they had quarreled. In order to get Lenore to study as she should, Sally had scolded, and Lenore had sometimes resented this. All of it together had made a bond between them, a good bond.

The important thing now, Sally knew, was not that she and Lenore might never see each other again. The important thing was that Lenore was going to a new school. She hadn't flunked out. And she wouldn't in the future.

Standing in the front doorway, looking after Lenore, Sally heard her mother calling to hurry her along with the household tasks that were waiting. She started toward the kitchen to tell her mother about Lenore. Then she realized that her mother must already know, for these things were part of her job at school. But she hadn't mentioned it. She had waited for Lenore to do the telling. Parents were amazing sometimes, Sally decided.

School was not the same without Lenore. Though it had not been easy to stay at Lenore's side after the news broke about her father, it seemed almost harder now that Lenore was gone. Except for Jonni, nobody seemed to act natural toward her. They were either cool, or too friendly, as if they could not forget her friendship with Lenore.

One day Jonni cornered Sally before the last period. "Sally, you've just got to join Girls' Club."

When Sally started to say it was too late now, Jonni shook her head vigorously. "We're having a membership drive. Haven't you seen the notices on the bulletin boards? We're having a money-raising campaign, and we need more girls to help. Come to the meeting with me after school."

Perhaps the club not only needed her. Perhaps she needed it very much right now, Sally decided. This was one of the times when it was handy having her mother right there in the school, in an office across the hall from the school library.

Her mother looked pleased at hearing that she was joining a club. "Have a good time," she said.

Rather to her surprise, she did have a good time. Also to her surprise, she was put on a committee. This meant there was work for her to do, but even the work seemed to be shaping up as fun.

She told Sue about it on Saturday, when once again Sue walked over to see her. First she apologized. "I hope you won't mind, Sue, but I'll have to clean my room while we talk. Otherwise I won't be through with my chores before it's time to go to Jonni's."

"Oh," Sue said, "are you going to Jonni's tonight?"

"With Myron and Judd," Sally said smugly.

Sue looked properly impressed. "I suppose all the girls go for Myron now. He really is great with a basketball." Then, as if fearing that she had been too generous toward a player from a rival school, Sue asked abruptly, "Whatever happened to that boy you were going to write to?"

It took a moment before she remembered the boy in Portland. "Oh, him. I decided it wasn't worth the effort. Besides, right now I'd never find the time."

She could restrain her big news no longer. "The Girls' Club is going to have a Hootenanny, Sue."

Sue looked envious. "Really? When? Can anybody go?"

"The fifteenth of next month." She laughed. "I'll be glad to sell you some tickets. It's to raise money for band uniforms and stuff like that. And, Sue, it was my idea! It just came to me all of a sudden, at club meeting. Most of the kids enjoy Hootenannys. Even those who can't dance can sing along and clap hands. So, I thought, why not cash in on it?"

Sue's eyes were wide. "You mean you've hired folk singers?"

"No. We couldn't afford that. Not this time, anyway. Our own kids will play instruments and lead the singing. What made me think of it is that Myron and Jonni are both so talented musically. They agreed to help, and so did some others. . . ."

She was so thrilled over the telling of how well everything was working out that she scarcely gave Sue a chance to talk, as she realized after Sue had gone home.

So the next Saturday, though she had many things to do, she decided to walk over to Sue's. Just for a little while. It was no more than fair, she decided, though she was sure now that things would never be quite as they used to be between them. And she suspected that Sue knew it, too.

The amazing thing about it was that she would not want to go back to the way things used to be—just the two of them, clinging to each other, shutting out, not only other people, but enriching experiences. She didn't want to go back to that, any more than she'd like to go back to old Hadley. And she wouldn't want to have missed knowing Lenore. And certainly not Jonni, for she hoped some day to be more like Jonni.

Sue was waiting at the door. But not for her, although she greeted her with an ecstatic, "Oh, Sally, I'm so glad you came today!" She went on to explain, "This is new car day for Whit! I've been waiting for him to drive up in his new car. I'm dying to see it."

Sue could talk of little else.

After a while Sally said apologetically that she just had to get home.

"Which one is it tonight?" Sue teased. "Myron or Judd?"

"Both." Sally laughed. "Plus Jonni. The four of us are going to the movies."

"I hope you have a good time," Sue said.

"You too," Sally responded.

She meant it and was happy in the assurance that Sue also meant it.

20

The Chosen One

Before she reached the corner on her way home, a chilling rain started to fall. It would be nice, she thought, pulling her scarf up to cover her hair, if Whit should come along and give her a ride.

And there he was, as if she'd conjured him up! His car was not brand-new, but it was a late model and shining clean from bumper to bumper.

He pulled the blue four-door to the curb and reached across to swing the right door open invitingly. "Hop in, Sally, and I'll give you a demonstration of how a car should ride and drive."

"Gladly," she said, "if you will promise to take me straight home. Much as I'd enjoy the full demonstration tour, I simply have to get straight home."

He looked rather startled at her answer. "It's a promise, but you don't know what you're passing up."

Settling herself in the seat beside him, Sally said, "I feel honored to be one of the first to ride in your new car, Whit."

"Not one of the first, Sally. The first." He sobered. "I guess you deserve the first ride. After all, it was your sister who gave me the clue—and a chance to redeem myself."

She didn't want him confessing to her. Not now, anyway. She managed to answer lightly, "If Lu gave you the clue, then I guess she is the one who deserves a ride."

"It's a deal," Whit said. "I'll be around—soon."

She was reaching for the door handle before the car rolled to a stop. The look on his face was more than she could bear.

Then she remembered something important. "You've heard about our benefit Hootenanny, I hope. If you'd like tickets, I have about a bushel to sell."

His laugh, that displayed two rows of fine white

teeth, lifted her spirits immensely.

"Tickets for the benefit of what or which?" he wanted to know.

"For the benefit of our school activities," Sally answered firmly.

His eyes were bright with admiration as he assured her, "When I stop around I just might buy part of that bushel. I guess maybe I owe it to your school."

"Maybe," she agreed readily. It didn't matter now that he knew that she knew about him. " 'Bye, Whit."

Her heart was light as she dashed through the drizzle and into the house. She laughed a little, just for the joy of laughing, as she saw that Lucia was lining up all the wastebaskets and was emptying those less full into those holding more.

"Whit has his new car," Sally told her sister. "And he says he's going to give you a ride in it soon because you gave him the clue about the carriage house. I guess I owe you an apology, Lu, because I never did really believe any of those things you said about the carriage house."

Lucia blushed with pleasure, and she murmured, "Oh, that's all right, Sally. Jeeks! Do you think Whit really will give me a ride?"

"I think he really will," Sally answered over her

shoulder as she headed to where she had left the vacuum cleaner.

"Oh, Sally," Lucia called after her, "I almost forgot! Mrs. Gruenwald says some people with older children have been looking at the Andres' house. They are very much interested in buying it, Mrs. Gruenwald said. . . ."

Sally almost answered with a groan, "This is where I came in!"

Mrs. Gruenwald again, and reports about new people for the carriage house!

Instead she answered cheerfully, "That's good," as she went on up the stairs.

A little later, as she started to turn on the vacuum cleaner in the upstairs hall, she saw that one of the two wastebaskets Lucia was about to carry to the trash burner held the treasured whip from out West.

"You're not burning Horace's whip?" she asked.

"Oh—it's broken," Lu answered somewhat sheepishly.

It wasn't really broken—just coming apart at the seams.

"Daddy could probably fix it," Sally suggested.

Lucia answered calmly, "I guess there's not much use hanging onto a horse whip when there's almost no chance that I will ever have a horse to use it on. Not unless we move from Linden. And I don't want to move from Linden. Do you?"

"Of course not. Not unless we had to." If they had to, she could do it more easily now than before she had changed high schools, of that she was sure.

As she watched Lucia march down the stairs, she struggled with a silly feeling of regret over the fact that Lu was growing out of childhood. Lu was ready to part with Horace. Her mother had said it would happen. All the same, it was hard to believe.

Just then it struck her. She could scarcely believe it. She had talked to Whit Fowler, not only without stammering and stuttering, but pretty much as she would have talked to Myron, or to Judd.

She sighed, a pleased sigh. It was going to be fun to ride again in Whit's car. It was going to be fun to go to the movies tonight, too. And it was fun having Myron wait to walk to school with her mornings. And it was fun having Judd tag after her as he often did at school. In fact, life these days was a great big lot of fun, including Girls' Club and serving on committees and thinking up ways to make money needed for school activities.

Supposing that Lu and Mrs. Gruenwald were right

about the Andres' house, it could be that another girl her age, or another boy, or both, would be moving in. And they would go to Hadley West.

She skipped back to the vacuum cleaner and turned it on once again. In a little while she started humming, and then, softly but fervently she began to chant:

"Hadley West!
Hadley West!
I'll be true and
Do my best."

Myron was right, of course. The way for her to be true to a school was to do her best and be a credit to the school. She was quite sure Judd thought she was a credit to their school. And as for Whit, unless she was very much mistaken he'd had a look of admiration on his handsome face.

She laughed softly. It was nice to know that a boy admired you. It gave a girl confidence in herself. She thought back to that day when she'd thought the sky had fallen in; the day when she learned that she would be going to the new school. Now it was hard to believe that she had been so upset about making the change.

She thought again of the boy or girl who might move into the Andres' house. Wouldn't it be something, she thought, if he—or she—or they—had the same qualms about going to a new school that she'd had?

If so, she might be able to point out a few things to them from her own experience. But just telling wouldn't be enough. She'd have to show them.

That was just one more thing to look forward to, she decided confidently as she pushed the vacuum cleaner ahead of her into the next room.